ONBOARD AND OFF LIMITS

LOUISA HEATON

MEDICAL ROMANCE

Recycling programs for this product may not exist in your area

ISBN-13: 978-1-335-99375-5

Onboard and Off Limits

Harlequin Enterprises ULC
22 Adelaide St. West, 41st Floor
Toronto, Ontario M5H 4E3, Canada
www.Harlequin.com

HarperCollins Publishers
Macken House, 39/40 Mayor Street Upper
Dublin 1, D01 C9W8, Ireland
www.HarperCollins.com

Printed in U.S.A.

1 2 3 4 5 6 7 8 9 10 HDC 28 27 26 25

No. It can't be!

His eyes met hers and he smiled at her and that smile was everything. For so long, Maddy had been telling herself that he'd never been as handsome as she remembered. That his smile was not as she kept imagining, but something she'd invented. She'd put him on a pedestal. Made him a god in her mind. Of course she was going to remember him as stunning. Dark, wolfish hair. Eyes twinkling in the med bay lights. He wore a trimmed beard now, that if anything, only served to make him more distinguished. Like he'd grown into himself and become the man he was always meant to be, rather than the young twenty-something he'd been before. And that smile...those lips... How many times had she kissed those lips? How many times had that mouth trailed over her expectant body? Dropping hot kisses onto tender skin?

He had sent that welcome basket.

It was her Nate.

He was here. On this ship.

Dear Reader,

I remember the excitement of going on my very first cruise ship holiday. Because I wasn't sure if I'd like it, we booked a small three-day cruise to France and back. I absolutely adored it, and since then, I have been on a lot of cruises! None around the Mediterranean, though, so that is where I decided I would send my hero and heroine, Maddy and Nate.

Cruises offer a world of possibilities, and I have always had the time of my life on them, so I knew that I wanted to give Maddy the time of her life on one, too! And what better than to give her a holiday romance with an old colleague who once broke her heart? Can she trust him this time? And will she ever find out the reason he vanished without a trace all those years before?

I hope you enjoy their story.

Bon voyage!

Louisa x

Louisa Heaton lives on Hayling Island, Hampshire, with her husband, four children and a small zoo. She has worked in various roles in the health industry—most recently four years as a community first responder, answering emergency calls. When not writing, Louisa enjoys other creative pursuits, including reading, quilting and patchwork—usually instead of the things she *ought* to be doing!

Books by Louisa Heaton

Harlequin Medical Romance

Christmas North and South

A Mistletoe Marriage Reunion

Cotswold Docs

Best Friend to Husband?
Finding a Family Next Door

Royal York Hospital

New Year to Nine-Month Surprise

Single Mom's Alaskan Adventure
Finding Forever with the Firefighter
Resisting the Single Dad Surgeon
The Surgeon's Relationship Ruse
One Night to Twin Miracle
Nurse's Night Before Valentine's

Visit the Author Profile page
at Harlequin.com for more titles.

Remembering Sheila Hodgson. Sorely missed x

CHAPTER ONE

'Oh my God. It's huge!' Dr Madeline Finch had just escaped the confines of the dock terminal at Southampton, where she'd spent a good hour going through her final bits of paperwork with the cruise line. She emerged in sunshine to stare at *Serendipity*, the brand-new ship sailing out to take its maiden voyage around the Mediterranean. This vessel, her home for the next six months, was a whole lot bigger than she thought it'd be. Her only experience of sailing had been on a canal boat many years ago, and one or two rowing boats when she'd studied at Cambridge, but this…behemoth…was still nothing like she'd ever imagined! She'd known that the ship was capable of carrying over four thousand passengers and nearly two thousand crew, of course, but to actually see it up close was like looking at a sailing city. Brilliant white, its name emblazoned in azure-blue, it towered above her so high, she had to shade her eyes to see right to the top.

'Wow.'

She let out a soft sigh. The nerves that had been held at bay whilst she'd dealt with some particularly headache-inducing paperwork a moment ago were now beginning to build again. What she was about to do was a spectacular pivot from her normal life. She'd always worked in busy, oftentimes dangerous, Accident and Emergency departments, but that part of her life was over, and now she was taking a new direction. She'd still be a doctor, but in an environment where it didn't need security guys standing ten feet away decked out in stab vests, ready and willing to protect the staff against patients. She'd been informed that life on board a cruise ship as a doctor, though still busy, would be much less dangerous than she had allowed herself to get used to—with the added benefit of good weather and beautiful destinations.

She could travel the world this way: live life, relax on beaches, explore cities. Have experiences that didn't result in her being attacked: a patient had lashed out when she'd refused them drugs. She'd taken time to recover from her surgery, and she had been given counselling, but the PTSD from the event had caused her to feel that she could not return to her old post at London Saint Hospital. Attempting to walk through those doors had caused such a significant panic attack, she'd ended up in her own department, surrounded by staff treating her as a patient as she'd breathed into a paper bag.

Her therapist had suggested a break and that she broaden her horizons—maybe take a busman's holiday, in which business could be mixed with pleasure. And, *serendipitously*, as she'd switched on her computer that day there'd been an email from Jenna, a friend with whom she'd gone to university. She'd extolled her new adventures on board a cruise ship that sailed around the Caribbean: how delightful it was; how relaxing and less *pressured*. She couldn't imagine working in an actual hospital ever again.

Maddy had looked up the cruise line's website, checked for vacancies and seen a posting for a doctor on the Venture Cruise Line's new flagship, *Serendipity*. In a moment of madness, she'd sent off an email, and now here she stood, about to board her new home and sail around the Mediterranean, stopping in ports such as Vigo, Port of Rome, Naples and Cagliari.

She'd never been to any of those places. She had only ever left the country once, going by train to Paris to enjoy a hen weekend with friends, and she'd never been able to remember much about it. This was going to be different—a whole new world. And a bright, wonderful new start to her professional and personal life.

This job was meant to help her recover from her trauma and ease her back into the world of work; it was meant to heal her wounds. Hopefully this ship, its people and its ports of call, would be just the ticket.

And maybe, just maybe, there might be a holiday romance: a Greek god with rippling abs; an Italian poet, perhaps? Or a Spanish *señor* who would whisk her onto a dance floor and then into his bed. Didn't she deserve something crazy like that, something carefree? Someone who would treasure her and treat her like a queen; who would blow her kisses and wave her goodbye as she sailed away with happy memories of their time together?

She'd told her therapist she was fed up being fearful, that life had to start getting better and she was going to make sweeping changes. So she'd left her old job, rented out her flat and decided to see the world. First, the Mediterranean for six months on this contract and, if it went well, then maybe she could message Jenna and see if she could get a posting on her ship on the other side of the Atlantic. She'd not seen her friend for so long.

Pulling her wheeled cases behind her, Maddy

began to make her way across the crew gangway. She gazed down at the water as she crossed, then up again at the boat, her anxiety making way for excitement, and was met on the other side by a crew member stood behind a small podium.

His name tag said he was Michele, and he was very handsome—olive-skinned and with a strong Italian accent. 'Welcome on board *Serendipity*; do you have your crew card?'

'Hi. Yes.' She pulled the ID card from her pocket and passed it over for him to scan.

'Dr Finch! Welcome to the family.'

'Thank you.'

He tapped away at his screen and then passed her some more paperwork she would read later. 'Your cabin is on deck three. Your ID card should open the door. Inside, you should find the itinerary and your onboarding schedule. *Bon voyage*!'

'Thank you.' She accepted back her ID and pulled her cases further into the ship, meeting with what seemed like an endless white corridor that turned this way and that, until she came to a set of stairs and a crew lift. She learned that she was on deck five and needed to go down two floors to find her cabin. She pressed the button for the lift and turned to smile at another crew member who'd arrived with her bags. 'Hi.'

'Hi. My name's Angie. I'm a singer in entertainment. You?'

'Maddy. Ship's doctor.' She shook Angie's hand.

'Oh, wow! Which deck are you heading to?'

'Three. Yourself?'

'I'm on deck two.'

The lift door slid open and they wheeled their bags and cases in and Maddy pressed the buttons for both floors. They arrived in a moment at deck three and the door pinged before it opened. 'Well, I'll see you around, I guess?' Maddy said.

'Mess deck hopefully, rather than in the medical bay!' Angie laughed as the door slid shut between them, giving her a quick wave before disappearing from sight.

Maddy turned. There were a couple of small signs indicating cabin numbers on the deck. Her cabin was 302 which, according to the sign, meant she should go left. She gave a nod of acknowledgement to people she met, smiled or said a hello back when one was offered, until she arrived at her cabin, stomach rolling with nerves. The ID card slid through the reader, the light changed from red to green, her door beeped and pushed open.

The cabin was larger than she'd expected. She'd looked at crew cabins online to see what she should expect and was happy to see that she had a single occupancy cabin. The living space had a bed as well as a sofa, a large desk with computer and monitor and some overhead shelving filled with a variety of medical textbooks. There was a fitted wardrobe that contained a small fridge at the bottom of it and a small chest of drawers upon which sat a tray with a kettle, two cups and an assortment of goodies with which she could make tea or coffee. A large porthole currently gave her a view of Southampton dock. There was also a door that led to a nice-sized bathroom and shower cabinet.

On the desk she noticed a small welcome basket: chocolate-chip muffins, some fruit and a card that read: *Welcome onboard! Nate x*

Weird. She'd known a Nate once, years ago as a junior doctor. It couldn't be him, though. There was more than one Nate in the world! Perhaps he was the cruise director or something and doctors just got a special welcome basket. Because, if it was the *other Nate*, well… It hadn't ended very well for her. In fact, he'd broken her heart when he'd left her without a word of explanation. Maybe this one here on *Serendipity* would be more reliable.

'Home sweet home!' She placed her cases off to one side and slid the messenger bag off her shoulders and onto the bed. There was a wad of papers—all the promised documents, a welcome pack and an onboarding schedule which would take place before they started letting on passengers tomorrow afternoon for setting sail at four-thirty p.m.

She almost couldn't believe she was here! There'd been an element of fantasy to the whole thing. She'd interviewed via video connection with Venture Cruise Line, the head office of which was in London. She'd filled in endless rounds of compliance paperwork, and ensured she had the relevant maritime medical training. There'd been a second in-person interview. It had all seemed so far away from the reality of the fact that she'd be soon living and working on board a huge, new cruise liner. A ship! She had no idea if she'd even get sea sick!

I guess I'll find out.

And now here she was, actually on board. Tomorrow they would set sail and her job would begin. She knew no-one here, and maybe that was a good thing. She could be whoever she wanted to be. She could be what she wanted others to see: a good, talented doctor. One who had quickly risen to become head of her Accident and Emergency department in London. One who was relaxed, friendly, confident. She would not let them see the doctor who was attacked and had PTSD. Or the doctor who had her heart broken after being abandoned by a guy she'd begun to fall in love with. Or the little girl she'd once been, hauled through the foster-care system. They wouldn't get to see any of that, or know that *Serendipity* was her chance to regain her confidence and put her past behind her.

She took some time to unpack, making her cabin a home, storing her cases under the bed. Then she sat at her desk for some time to familiarise herself with the onboarding schedule. She was due at the medical bay, which was equipped with its own laboratory and radiography equipment, tomorrow morning at nine for a tour of the medical bay and a meet-and-greet with her new colleagues. And then they would go through the submitted medical information of the crew and passengers. At two o'clock, there would be a crew clinic and then the day schedule would change once the passengers arrived and shift work would begin.

She was excited about it; ready to get back to work and to get her teeth back into the whole reason she'd got into medicine in the first place: to help people; to heal people...including herself.

Dr Nathaniel Blake wasn't used to feeling nervous. It was a strange state to find himself in.

During a job interview once, someone had asked him to use three words to describe himself and he'd answered confident, decisive and passionate. Confident and decisive, because he moved through the world assuredly. He wasn't a man who dithered. He wasn't a man who questioned his own decisions. He thought through problems, made a decision and then executed it without doubt. He'd chosen passionate because he was passionate about his job. Passionate about his work, about being a good doctor and making choices for patients that were right for them.

So, the fact that he'd woken that morning feeling incredibly edgy and nervous was not a comfortable feeling for him to experience, and it was all because Dr Madeline Finch—dear Maddy—was on board.

Serendipity was a new ship for him to be on, but this was not his first contract as a cruise-ship doctor with Venture Cruise Lines. He'd worked on their ships *Decadence* and *Pacific*, the last of which had been with his brother, Lucas. His brother was on *Serendipity*, too, as an ice dancer. They walked through this world together again. There'd been a time when it had not been like this and he valued every minute they got to be together.

But Maddy… Maddy was from his past, from

when he'd worked in a busy, fast and frenetic London Accident and Emergency department. Both of them had been brand-new junior doctors at the time and there'd been so much going on, so much to learn, so much to understand, so much responsibility and so many patients; he'd been overwhelmed and it had caused him to turn to Maddy for comfort. Friends with benefits, they'd agreed, and she had been amazing—just the release he'd needed at the end of a long day of pressure and worry. Maddy had been the welcoming arms when he turned up at her door, and later the hot vixen between the sheets, allowing him to forget the pressures of their jobs and their lives for an hour or two.

Just thinking about those nights... *Wow.* They had been intense! She had needed the release just as much as he had, and he had many fond memories of sex in all kinds of places! They'd done it up against a wall—worth a try at least once, but only if they didn't mind having terrible leg ache the next day when they had a long twelve-hour shift to get through. They'd had sex in his car—not enough room, but fun—and, once, sex in an empty patient room in the hospital, with no locks on the door and extremely risky every time they heard footsteps getting closer. But they'd had fun. Lots and lots of no-strings, adult fun.

But then he'd received the telephone call that had changed everything and he'd had to leave—immediately. First, taking holiday that had been owed to him, then getting in touch with the hospital and letting them know that he would not be coming back. He'd been needed elsewhere, a family matter. And, though it had pained him to know that he didn't have a chance to say goodbye to Maddy, he'd hoped that she would understand. After all, it wasn't as if they'd been involved or anything. No strings, friends with benefits—that had been all. He'd owed her nothing.

And yet...he'd felt bad, leaving without a word, not even a telephone call or an email. It wasn't the honourable thing to do, but he'd not been thinking straight at the time. His family matter had consumed him to begin with, but then, as time had become more his own, he'd thought how upset she'd be with him for just going like that. But too much time had passed to contact her and he'd just thought it would be easier somehow to maintain no contact. What would he have been able to offer her anyway except for sex? It would only have dragged up again any hurt she might have felt at him leaving. And so he kept it no contact—decision made.

You're no good anyway—just what Bill used to tell him.

And then he'd arrived on board and received a list of his new medical crew, his new colleagues. Some he knew from previous ships, but among the new doctors coming on board was a name that had stood out straight away: Dr Madeline Finch. And he'd known, in an instant, that *this* maiden voyage was going to be crazy with her here.

Hopefully, she would be fine about it. Hopefully, there would be peace between them—friendship, acceptance. They were both adults, more mature than they'd been eight years ago when he'd left.

He'd not wanted her to be surprised by his being there, by being her boss, so he'd sent a welcome basket. A little heads up. It had seemed the decent thing to do. He'd faltered on communication before; he would start off right here.

Because there'd be no real reason for her to hold a grudge, right?

It had just been sex—hot and heavy sex. They owed each other nothing.

CHAPTER TWO

MADDY WOKE REFRESHED the next morning, after an early night. Yesterday, she'd gone for a walk around the ship, trying to familiarise herself with the layout, what was on each deck and how to access all the crew corridors, stairs and lifts. The ship was like two cities: the one above, where the passengers existed, lived and enjoyed whatever the ship had to offer; and the one below, where the crew lived and ate and had their own entertainment areas.

She'd found one of the two crew mess areas, grabbed a bite to eat and chatted with a few new friends. She'd met Laila, who had travelled over from France and was a singer; Maribel, from Finland, who was a chef; and Bogdan from Poland, who was there as a cruise director. Everyone had seemed nice and Maddy had done her best to project positivity, confidence and welcome, with no sign of the woman who just a year ago had been almost too afraid to leave her house in case she had a panic attack.

Thankfully, there'd been no sign of anyone from her past. That welcome basket, signed '*from Nate x*,' had niggled at the back of her brain and she'd almost not gone to the crew mess at all, in fear that somehow the man who years ago had unwittingly claimed her heart might be onboard this very ship. But then she'd given herself a very stern talking to in the mirror. The likelihood of him being here was miniscule! And was she really going to hide away in her cabin because he might be there? Ridiculous! She was a grown woman, and besides he wouldn't be on this ship; there had to be thousands of people around the world called Nate and it was simply a coincidence, that was all.

Today, she dressed in dark trousers and a fitted white blouse, and hung her ID lanyard around her neck. Standing in front of the mirror, she took some time to twist and pin up her long red hair and she applied a little make-up, but not too much, smiling at her reflection, proud of how far she had come.

You can do this.

She knew the nerves would go soon enough. Once she was busy, everything would be fine; it was just this bit, hanging around, waiting, anticipating, imagining. There was no reason for her to be nervous. She was an experienced doctor. There would be no drug addicts on board looking to score meds from her. She just had butterflies because it had been a long, long time since she'd had to experience a first day on a job.

Maddy thought back to her first day at London Saint Hospital. She'd been so excited, so nervous! Her legs had felt like jelly and she'd been so keen to get down to working with patients. Of course, it hadn't turned out to be like anything she'd imagined. There'd been almost a whole week of induction, sitting in lecture rooms listening to their bosses and educators talk them through hospital policies that she'd already studied at home. She'd found herself turning to the guy sat next to her when he'd yawned at the same time as her and they'd smiled at one another. He'd had a spark in his eyes and he'd been cute!

Nathaniel, but everyone calls me Nate.

Madeline, but everyone calls me Maddy.

They'd stuck to each other's sides like glue at the beginning. If there'd been something one of them wasn't sure about, they'd turned to the other in hope of an answer before going to a superior, if need be. That closeness had become a friendship, that spark in their eyes an attraction. It had been exciting, thrilling, and, after that first time together in the folly,

Maddy had laughed, resting her head against his chest, sweat coating her body in a delightful way. She'd imagined that this could really be something, when he'd said, *We don't need the pressures of a relationship, what with everything else going on, so we should just do the friends with benefits thing—what do you think?*

His words had been a bucket of cold water on her hopes. But she'd *liked* him, really liked him. And she'd figured, if she just agreed, then she'd keep getting to hang around him, be close and experience the physicality that they shared. And she'd so wanted to seem cool with it. So wanted to seem as if she could just roll with anything and not feel that she might not be enough to be anything more. So she'd agreed, hoping that maybe one day he would change his mind. She'd simply nodded, smiled and straightened her clothes before they'd returned to the party.

It was only later she realised what a mistake it had been because, whilst it had been 'no strings' for him, she'd very much felt that there *were* strings. She'd begun to have feelings for him—strong feelings. Ones that she'd secretly kept inside, hoping that one day he would turn to her in bed and tell her that he was actually falling in love with her, the way she was with him. She'd put him on a pedestal, but she should have known she'd never be able to reach him up there.

But, then again, she'd always had an active imagination.

Maddy checked her watch. It was nearly time. Probably best to get there early, make a good first impression and seem keen, eager. And she was! Even though her nervousness at being back in a medical setting niggled at her with all the 'what if?'s—*what if a passenger had too much to drink and got aggravated?*—she left her cabin and pushed through. She'd spent enough hours in therapy to know that it was just anxiety, her PTSD.

I need to face my fears. See some patients, prove to myself that I'm safe.

The thin corridors were busy in the bowels of the ship with crew members wearing uniforms and in casual clothes, going this way and that. There was an energy to everyone this morning. Today passengers would come onboard, and tonight they would set sail from Southampton and head towards their first port—Vigo, in north-west Spain.

She saw Bogdan and gave him a wave as he headed up some stairs dressed in a very posh suit, his hair slicked back. She took the stairs down to deck two, where the medical bay was located. She wasn't sure what to expect. Would it be tiny, quiet?

She saw a woman in a nurse's uniform head in and she turned to hold the door for Maddy. 'Thanks.'

The nurse gave her a nod. 'Hi. Genevieve. Nice to meet you.'

'Maddy. Nice to meet you too.'

There was a reception area, staffed by a woman whose hair was so tightly pulled back into a dark bun, her face looked taut. 'Good morning,' she said, standing to reach out with her hand to say hello. 'I'm Sylvia.'

'Genevieve—nurse.'

'Madeline—doctor.'

Sylvia cross-checked their names against a clipboard. 'Ah, yes! Excellent. Everyone else has arrived. Come with me and I'll take you to the staff room for induction.'

A cloud of sweet-smelling, floral perfume seemed to follow in Sylvia's wake as she led them down a small corridor towards a room at the end, swinging the door wide and holding it open for them. Genevieve went through first and dipped right to head for a spare chair. Maddy assumed she would just follow her, but as she stepped into the room, her gaze went to a guy standing at the front of the room and she felt her steps falter.

She was unable to tear her gaze away from the man standing there. Her mouth was dry, her heart pounding.

No. It can't be!

His eyes met hers and he smiled at her and that smile was *everything*. For so long, she'd told herself that he'd never been as handsome as she remembered. That his smile was *not* as she kept imagining, but something she'd invented. She saw his dark, wolfish hair, his eyes twinkling in the medical bay lights. He wore a trimmed beard now, that if anything only served to make him more distinguished. It was as if he'd grown into himself and become the man he was always going to be, rather than the young twenty-something he'd been before. And that smile…those lips… How many times had she kissed those lips? How many times had that mouth trailed over her expectant body, dropping hot kisses onto tender skin?

He had sent that welcome basket. It was *her* Nate. He was here, on this ship.

'Maddy, come over here, there's a seat.' Genevieve called to get her attention.

Somehow, she tore her gaze away, tried to control her beating heart and, blushing, made her way over to the nurse at the back of the room and sat down.

It felt as if her cheeks were on fire. Her whole

body tingled with adrenaline and she realised her legs were trembling, and she wanted to run.

This was meant to be her fresh start. This was meant to be a place where she could be the new and improved Dr Madeline Finch—a doctor not haunted by what had happened to her in the past.

But her past was *here*.

The man who'd unknowingly broken her heart was her new boss!

CHAPTER THREE

THE FIRST DAY onboarding new crew and getting to know his new team was always an exciting day for Nate and this was the first time he'd be the team lead on board. He felt the weight of the responsibility for all the crew and passengers, and wanted to show Venture Line Cruises that he was capable and would do a fine job as Chief Medical Officer. But all the excitement he'd been feeling, all that apprehension, went right out of the porthole the second Maddy appeared in the doorway and saw him for the first time since he'd left London Saint.

She looked *amazing*, as she always had. Her rich, auburn hair contrasted with the beautiful creaminess of her skin, still delightfully freckled. Her eyes were blue and sky-bright. The gloss on her lips drew his attention to her mouth, and the way her lips had parted in surprise at seeing him. Was it surprise? He'd sent that welcome basket. Hadn't she realised it was from him? Because she'd looked shocked and then her cheeks had coloured. Genevieve, with whom he'd worked with on *Pacific*, called her over and Maddy edged her way through a row of people to go and sit with her, almost hiding at the back.

So…not a pleasant surprise for her. That was a little disconcerting. He'd hoped that they'd both be able to put the past exactly where it belonged and move forward. They'd got on brilliantly last time, and he'd enjoyed the many occasions when they'd found each other on short breaks to talk through what has been happening with their patients. If her mentor had been just as bad as his, she'd had a sympathetic ear. She'd been someone with whom he could share a joke or take some space if a patient hadn't made it—someone who'd told him that everything was okay.

Maddy had been by his side since the beginning of his journey as a doctor. He hoped that she would stand by his side just as steadfastly now and help him lead this department so that they got through this voyage, and all the ones to follow, with the support he knew she could give him.

'Good morning, everyone. To those I haven't worked with before, my name is Nathaniel Blake and I will be the Chief Medical Officer on board the *Serendipity*. We have three other new doctors joining us for the next six months, Dr Muhammed Bedi, Dr Theo Galanis and Dr Madeline Finch—if you'd all like to stand and make yourselves known?'

They all stood and smiled, or raised a hand in greeting to their new crewmates, but his gaze couldn't help but go to Maddy. She looked uncomfortable, blushing, but she'd never been one to enjoy the spotlight.

After they sat down, he explained rotas and shift patterns, responsibilities and duties, pairing one new doctor with an experienced one. Behind him on a screen was a floor layout, like a blueprint for the medical bay, and he went through it briefly, detailing where everything was, giving everyone the codes for doors and utility rooms, explaining what sort of equipment they had and what levels of treatment they could provide on board *Serendipity*. He went through some safety procedures and fire-drill procedures and explained where their muster stations were, in case the ship had to be evacuated.

Once he was done, he announced the shifts. 'Dr Finch? You'll be working with me on day shifts to begin with.'

Once the briefing was completed and everyone dismissed, he waited for everyone to filter out so he could speak to the only member of staff left behind. If he were being honest, he'd thought she might try and escape with the others.

Nate was left looking at a rather uncomfortable Maddy in the staff room. 'Hey.'

'Hey.'

'It's good to see you, after all this time.'

She stood, straightening her clothes and forcing a smile. 'I guess we ought to get started? The briefing mentioned that we should be checking the medical histories the crew and passengers have provided.'

All business, then. 'Of course. We'll head to my office. After you.' He stepped back so she could go past him towards the door.

But she didn't come to the front to go past him. She stayed in the back row and edged past the chairs and towards the door. When she got there, she turned to face him. 'Did you pick me to be on the same shift as you because of what we had?'

As the images of their nights together flooded his memory at her prompting, he felt his pulse increase and felt a surge of awareness for her: their bodies writhing in the dark; the way she bit her lower lip and arched her back, her hands scrunching the bedsheets. He smiled. 'No. Venture Line Cruises picked you for the day shift because that was what you told them you'd prefer.'

He saw her think about it, realising the truth of his words, and then she blushed again. 'Right.'

Did she wish now that she'd asked for a night shift, or to be one of the part-timers who covered weekends and illnesses in the senior medical staff? Because, if so, that was disappointing. He'd hoped they could put what had happened between them, in the past where it belonged. He was keen to see what kind of doctor she was now. Before, they'd both been juniors, uncertain and not yet confident in every decision. He'd grown a lot in the intervening years since he'd last seen her; he'd had to. Had she?

Nate stepped up close to her in the doorway, inhaled the soft perfume she was wearing and felt his senses go dizzy. She still had a certain physical effect on him, that was for sure.

'This way…'

His office was the size of Maddy's cabin and she found herself looking around it with a careful eye as she stood just inside the doorway and Nate went to his desk. He dragged another chair over from its position against the wall and stood behind it, his hands on its back.

'Take a seat.' He smiled at her, that beautiful smile of his, that she'd seen so many times in her dreams. A smile that had once haunted her, which she'd thought she'd never get to see again. And yet here she was, in an office with him. He was so different, and yet the same and she had to fight with every fibre of her being not to gush, run into his arms and tell him how happy she was to see him.

She was happy in one way: he wasn't dead, at least! She'd had no idea about what had happened when he'd left without a word. There'd been gossip after he'd gone; of course there had. People had speculated—mostly the other juniors, but then the senior team had sat them all down and told them that there'd been a family matter and that was the end of it.

'A family matter' could have been anything. And, as she'd sat there in that small room at London Saint, Maddy had realised that she knew absolutely nothing about his family, because he'd never spoken about them. They'd not spoken about personal matters at all. It had all been work. And sex—lots and lots of sex.

But she'd also been angry, angry at him leaving without a word. Could he not have sent her an explanatory text or an email? Couldn't he have called her? Hadn't she deserved that? Or had he thought so little of her, when she'd thought so much of him?

And she was angry at herself now, for asking for day shifts.

She gave him a look that suggested she would not sit down until he had stepped away from the chair, which he did with a small smile, settling into his own chair and waiting for her to join him.

'It's good to see you, Maddy.'

'Only friends get to call me Maddy,' she said, still standing by the doorway.

He nodded. 'You're upset?'

'Of course I am!'

'Well, I understand, of course, but that was a long time ago, and it's in the past now. We are here to do a job, and time is ticking, so shall we move forward and go through these medical histories, so we're both familiar?'

So, no apology, then; still no explanation. Did she not deserve either? How could she have got their relationship so wrong? 'Fine, let's just get on with it.' She settled herself down into her chair, adjusting its position so that it wasn't as close to him as he'd initially placed it, and gazed at the screen.

Nate began going through the more notable medical histories of the crew that were onboard *Serendipity*—nothing too major, but just conditions to be aware of. Generally most of the crew were young and in good health. Some of the passengers embarking the ship had a few more serious things to be aware of, and Nate ran through them with her as best he could, whilst she sat and nodded, choosing not to say much—because why should she, if he wasn't going to say much to her either?

'We become a family on board, Maddy. Sorry… Madeline. It doesn't work unless we do. We're confined together on board for six months and we have to have each other's backs.'

She stood, then turned to face him. 'How can I have the back of someone who abandoned me?'

'I was in an impossible situation. If it helps, it wasn't about you.'

No. It didn't help. 'Did you not think to call me? Not even once?'

'I did.'

'And?'

Nate sucked in a deep breath, then let it out. 'Too much time had passed. I thought it might be too little, too late, so I just…let it go. I never thought I'd see you again. I thought you'd just move on, and that was probably for the best anyway. I mean, look at you! You look amazing; you must be doing well?'

If only he knew about all that she had been through! If only he had been by her side, she might have got through her trauma easier!

Would he have sat by her bed and held her hand? Made her laugh with his bawdy jokes as she recovered? Would he have stopped her from being attacked in the first place? They'd always seemed to have some sort of extra-sensory perception when the other needed support.

Maddy felt barely restrained tears prick the backs of her eyes and hated herself for getting emotional. It simply wouldn't do! She sniffed and checked her watch. He didn't deserve to see her cry. He didn't deserve to hear about her life, not any more. From now on, she was going to keep it purely professional between them, even if her body did still stir at being close to him. Even if it did yearn to push aside all the unresolved anger she had from his disappearance years ago and just rush into his arms.

She pushed down her desire to touch him, to hold him. She focused on how she'd bristled when he'd mentioned that they were *family* here. Anger would get her through this. It always had. 'Staff clinic starts at two?'

He nodded.

'I'll see you then.'

Ysabel Demetriou came limping into the crew clinic that afternoon, wincing and favouring her left leg. But she was smiling as she came into

Nate's consultation room and lowered herself slowly into a chair.

'How can I help you today?'

'I've hurt my ankle and I need you to look at it for me. Hopefully, it's just a sprain.'

'Okay; what were you doing that caused you to hurt it?'

'I'm an ice-dancer, and I was doing a warm-up on the ice just before lunch and took a fall doing a triple lutz. Stupid, really. I always nail them, but I think I landed funny.'

'Did you use the correct edge of your skate?'

She smiled at him. 'You know skating?'

'My brother is an ice-dancer here on board. I've watched him practise often enough and heard him speak about it. You pick up on things,' he said, shrugging.

'What's his name?'

'Lucas.'

'Oh, Lucas! Yes, I met him last night.'

'Okay. Otherwise, fit and well? You didn't bang your head during the fall?'

'All good and no, no head injury. I got straight back up and carried on. It's only since then that the ankle is really hurting and I've got a show tomorrow night that I need to be in. I've got a solo skate and so I need to be on point.'

'No dizziness beforehand?'

Ysabel shook her head.

'Alright. Let's take a look at this ankle, then, shall we?' Nate got up from behind his desk and indicated she should get up onto the examination bed.

She was wearing joggers, socks and trainers, so he was able to see both ankles easily side by side. Her right ankle did look a little puffier than the left, but not by much. He palpated the ankle, foot and lower leg and then began to rotate and test the ankle joint to gauge the range of movement and the patient's pain level.

The ankle itself moved how he expected it to move, though clearly it was sore for Ysabel. 'Does it hurt all the time, or only when you bear weight on it?'

'All the time. A bit worse when I step on it, but not much.'

'Okay. I think you've got a mild sprain. I definitely don't think you've broken anything. So what I'm going to recommend is that you follow the usual procedures for an injury like this. You're going to do five things. Protect your ankle, so wear your boots. I want you to rest the ankle as much as possible and apply an ice pack for up to twenty minutes at a time. Wear a compression bandage around the ankle during the day and try to keep the ankle elevated as much as possible ahead of tomorrow's show. Do you have a stand-in?'

'Yes,' Ysabel said, grudgingly. 'But this is my first solo dance in a lead role. It's important. I can't let someone else take what I've worked so hard for.'

'I understand, but your health comes first. No point in pushing through and ruining your ankle so that you can't skate again. I want you to rest and take it easy. Take painkillers if you need to. Do you have any?'

'Of course. Is paracetamol okay?'

'Absolutely. Promise me you'll rest until tomorrow and maybe try a skate in the afternoon; see how you go and make a decision then?'

'Fine. Maybe you could come and watch the show? Hopefully I won't need you, but it'd be nice to know you were ringside.'

Nate sighed and smiled. 'Okay. I'll try, but only if you promise me that if it feels worse, you will let your stand-in do the show.' He held out his hand.

Ysabel eyed it and then shook his hand. 'Deal.'

The nurses triaged the patients first as they arrived to clinic. It was a similar system to how it worked in an Accident and Emergency department and Maddy liked that, because she knew then that there wasn't anyone sitting in a waiting room who really ought to be seen straight away. Thankfully, it being the embarkation day and with everyone new to the ship, there weren't actually that many patients at all. She'd noted that Nate was seeing a query sprained ankle and she'd been called to one of the bays because one of the ship's chefs had got a nasty burn to his hand.

It was her first patient since the attack. It was the only reason her mouth was so dry, her palms sweaty and her stomach rolling as if they were already at sea.

Paolo Conti sat on the examination bed in the bay when she entered, with his hand resting in a bowl of water, and a huge frown on his face. The nurse had written that the burn wasn't serious, and that Paolo had not even wanted to come to the medical bay, but Venture Cruise Lines had a very strict policy on injuries received whilst on board, no matter how minor. They all got reported and each injury had to be seen by a medic.

Before she pulled open the curtain, Maddy centred herself by taking a huge breath.

I can do this.

She painted on a smile of greeting and pulled open the curtain.

'I am fine,' he said, his voice filled with irritation before she'd even walked in. 'Honestly, look.' He lifted his hand from the water, moving it, twisting it this way and that, scrunching his hand to show a full range of movement. His mood, however, was unhappy. 'It does not hurt all that much any more. Can I go back to the kitchens?'

Maddy hesitated, sensing his antagonism straight away, her blood pounding through her system in an instant alert. This was not what she'd expected from her first patient. The desire to flee reared up, but she'd been preparing for this. It wasn't going to happen again, but she kept her distance by the curtain. 'I need to assess the injury, Mr Conti. How did it happen?'

'How you think? In the kitchen! I tell the nurse this already!' he said, voice raised.

Maddy put up both hands in a placatory way, trying to calm him, her heart pounding, sensing the potential danger, backing away to her exits. 'I understand, but I'm going to need you to calm down.' Adrenaline was coursing through her. She wanted to run. She'd faced an angry patient before and it had not ended well for her.

'I am calm!'

'Sir, I need you to—'

'What's going on in here?' Suddenly Nate was there, behind her, looking at Mr Conti and then stepping between him and Maddy.

She felt relief flood her system that someone else was there to help her deal with the patient, but why did it have to be Nate? Now he was going to think her incompetent in handling a difficult patient. She touched Nate's arm and instantly regretted it. A frisson of electricity shot up her arm. She had to take back control! 'It's fine. Mr Conti is impatient to get back to work, that's all.'

Nate turned to look at her, then back at Paolo. 'You will lower your tone when you speak to my staff, is that understood?'

For a moment, there was a standoff. The much bigger, angrier chef, staring at the cooler, calmer, collected Nate. There must have been something in Nate's gaze that had the chef nodding and backing down, holding his other hand up in surrender. 'My apologies. Onboarding day is a busy day for the buffet and I am needed in the kitchen.'

Nate turned to her. 'Are you alright?'

'Yes.' It was difficult to meet his gaze. Earlier she had been so angry with him and now... Well, she was still angry, but he had just come to her rescue, and she was embarrassed by it, yet grateful. It was a weird set of emotions to feel all at once. 'Thank you.'

'I'll be in my office. I'll leave the door and this curtain open,' he said, directing the last part at Paolo as Nate walked away.

Maddy watched him go, feeling a little disconcerted. ‘Accidents in the kitchen are easily done, but you did the right thing by putting your hand in water.’ She gave him a hesitant smile as she put on some gloves to examine his hand. ‘May I?’ There was redness to the skin, but no blisters, no swelling. ‘Can you feel me touching you here? And here?’

Paolo nodded.

‘Does it feel tight?’

‘No.’

‘Pain?’

‘Little. I’ve had worse.’

‘Alright. Well, you should be fine, but if you get blisters you must come back and see me, alright? We’ll cover the burn so you can return to work, but any sign of infection, or difficulty moving the hand and fingers, you come back for that as well. Take painkillers if you need to.’

‘Thank you. I can go now?’

‘In a minute.’ Maddy helped him pat dry his hand and then covered it in cling film, knowing he would be returning to the kitchen and handling food. ‘Okay. Be careful, alright?’

‘Thank you. And…my apologies. For earlier.’

She gave him a quick nod, letting out a big breath once the fiery chef had gone. He was a big guy, much bigger than her. She stood five foot seven; Paolo had to have been at least six feet or more, easily—solidly built, too.

She headed to a computer terminal to write up his notes, swiping her card to access the system and then noting the way her fingers trembled as they hovered over the keys.

This was not the start she'd hoped for by coming to work on a cruise ship. They'd not even left Southampton dock yet and already she'd been quaking in her boots! If it hadn't been for Nate, then… No, it would have been fine. Paolo was just frustrated, that was all.

Why am I making excuses for him? Because I always do.

Even when she'd been attacked before, she'd tried to excuse the guy. It hadn't been his fault, because he'd been an addict. It hadn't been his fault, because he'd been in pain. It hadn't been his fault, because he'd been in withdrawal. If she hadn't have got in his way…

Maddy made fists with her hands, then relaxed them, imagining all the stress leaving her body, the way her therapist had suggested. She looked up over the console and down the corridor towards the end, where Nate's office was. He'd not hesitated. He'd come straight to her assistance, as she imagined he'd do for any of his team. She put everything into the notes, including Nate's intervention, just in case. Then she got up and walked towards his office, hesitating by the door before rapping her knuckles on the wood to get his attention.

Nate looked up.

'I just wanted to thank you. For just now.'

'No problem. Are you alright, Madeline?'

Looking at him right now was so hard to do! She just wanted to run into his arms and have him hold her. Feel him in her embrace once again. Breathe him in. But it had been so long. She had no idea whether he was still single, or married, or involved with someone. They could even be on this boat! It could be one of the nurses! Who knew! Not that she could ever get involved with a man like Nate ever again. He'd broken her heart once, she'd be a fool to give him the opportunity to do so again. She would have to keep her distance.

She nodded. 'Yes. I just needed to say thanks, that's all.'

'You're very welcome.' He smiled. A smile that clutched at her heart, just like it had all those years ago. A smile that left her helpless. Vulnerable. He could have asked her anything with that smile back in the day and she would have done it. Run away with him? Yes. A hundred times yes. Did he know the power his smile had on her?

'I guess you can call me Maddy.' It was an olive branch.

He nodded.

Because he was right. They *had* to work together on this cruise for at least six months. That was how long her contract was and she wasn't entirely sure how long she could be mad at him. Not now that he was here. Back in her life. Just as charmingly irresistible as he'd been before, being all heroic and coming to her rescue and protecting her, like she was a damsel in distress.

He could never know how much that meant to her.

'Do you have a moment?' Nate had gone looking for Maddy and found her at the reception desk, talking to Sylvia, their receptionist.

Delightfully, her cheeks flushed with colour at seeing him, but he knew she had nothing to do and at that moment, and neither did he. Crew consultations were over and an important moment was coming up.

'Sure. What's up?'

He smiled. 'Come with me.' He wished they had the old easy association in which he could have just taken her hand, but they weren't who they used to be any more.

Nate led her away from the medical bay, down the corridor and over to a crew lift that would take them up to the promenade deck.

'The *Serendipity* is about to leave Southampton. You don't want to miss the sail-away party,' he said as they emerged into the sunshine and they saw all the people who had gathered. Music was being played, and crew members were dancing, trying to get passengers to join in. He walked her over to the railing and they looked down at Southampton dock. He knew no-one there—his only family was on board—but still he waved.

'Who are you waving to?' Maddy asked.

'Anybody.'

She looked at him as if he was crazy. 'Are all your goodbyes this weird? Or just the ones I get not to witness?'

He laughed. He wasn't going to get pulled into an argument about how he hadn't said goodbye to her. That was in the past—a very painful past. 'It's called living in the moment. You should try it!'

The ship's horn sounded, long and loud, and slowly the ship began to move away from the quay.

'We're off!' He beamed at her. 'Go on! Wave!'

'I have no-one to wave to.'

'Do you think all these people do? Those are dock workers down there, sailors. It's not their family members, but they wave anyway; it's what you do on board. It's all part of the fun. Come on—wave. Smile. Enjoy!'

Maddy sighed, but lifted her hand and began to wave, rather half-heartedly at first, as if she was embarrassed, but then as the ship pulled further and further away she really seemed to get into it.

He stole glances at her when she wasn't looking, his heart aching for all that he had lost with her. Could they have been something more than a hot fling? It was a real possibility. He could have fallen hard for this woman and, though something horrible had pulled him from her orbit, he was also grateful for the family crisis that had got him out of a tight spot. Because he'd not been ready for her. He'd not deserved her good, kind heart and there'd been moments between them when he'd felt that she was beginning to develop feelings for him, and that had scared the living crap out of him. He'd been so isolated for so long then along had come Maddy, swimming out to his island in the middle of an ocean and encouraging him to swim back with her to land.

But there'd been a reason he'd been isolated, a reason he'd been stranded, and the truth was, he'd stranded himself—because relationships with people he'd cared for had all been destroyed. He wasn't going to destroy Maddy, so he'd kept her at arm's length and told her they could only be friends with benefits, because that was all he'd been able to give.

He was in a different place now, but he had no idea where she was. Maybe she was settled. Maybe she had a love waiting for her somewhere. Maybe she wasn't as alone as she had been before. That had been part of the attraction back then—they'd been two lonely, hurt people, salving each other's wounds with sex, sex and more sex. Hot, passionate sex—almost as if they'd been starved of affection all their lives and were hungry for touch and connection.

They'd had a lustful thing going on and so it was understandable why his body reacted to her presence once again. It knew what she was capable of making him feel. It craved her, like a drug. But, until he knew her situation, he would be the perfect gentleman.

Behind them, the holiday music blaring out from the speakers on board filled their ears, and when a song came on that he absolutely adored he touched her arm and indicated she should follow him. He led her down some steps and out onto the deck where the entertainment crew was dancing near the swimming pools and hot tubs. He waded into the group and began to dance, crooking his finger at her to join him, laughing and calling her name.

Maddy stood there, blushing and shaking her head. 'No way! I can't do that!'

'Come on! Let yourself go for a moment!' She'd always been highly strung. The only time he'd ever seen her let go of her inhibitions was when they'd been intimate. She'd become a different person when she'd got dressed. It was as if she'd been putting on a mask and costume to be someone else. Who had been the real Madeline Finch? Was she still all buttoned up?

Nate rolled his hips, swaying this way and that. A passenger joined him, a young woman in a short sun dress, and he took her hand and twirled her round. He really wanted Maddy to join in, but the next time he looked for her she had gone, disappearing into the crowd, and he felt his heart sink, even if outwardly he maintained his smile for everyone else and carried on dancing.

Lying on the bed in her cabin, Maddy pressed the heels of her hands into her eyes and groaned out loud in frustration. How could one man still hold such sway over her emotions, even after all this time?

He seemed full of abundant joy, confident and sure of himself—whereas she still felt as if she were that young junior doctor, afraid, uncertain, still finding her way in a world that seemed keen to keep beating her down and holding her prisoner with all her fears and doubts.

Watching Nate smile and wave to the dock workers had been one thing, but then to see him joyfully join the dancers, moving his hips in that provocative way, feeding off of the energy and happiness of others… Maddy had felt so jealous of that woman he'd danced with, the way she'd twirled in his arms and then had drawn close to salsa, pressing her body against his, her skirt swishing around her perfectly tanned thighs and elegant legs, so sure of her body, oozing confidence. *Why can't I be like that? Why can't I just let loose?*

They'd looked good together, Nate and the passenger. How was she going to keep their relationship totally professional if he was going to do things like that? *I cannot fall for him again!*

He made it so easy, though. He was the type of guy who opened his arms wide for her and welcomed her in. He was easy on the eye, too. He could have gone for lots of women at that hospital. Plenty had made it clear that they were up for some fun with him, if he so desired, but he had never looked beyond her. Despite the fact that they'd been only friends with benefits and had no claim on each other, he'd only ever slept with her, and she with him.

And he'd been perfect! She remembered one

night when he'd driven them out to Surrey and they'd gone to this perfect little village pub and sat outside in the pub garden. There was a small river that ran along the bottom of it, dotted with ducks and two resident swans. She and Nate had sat with their backs against a wooden bench, staring out over the water, his arm casually resting around her shoulders. She'd leaned in and rested her head on his shoulders in this perfect moment, and she had felt him turn to kiss the top of her head. It had been a warm summer's evening. The air had been thick with the scent of honeysuckle and jasmine, and in that moment she had felt wanted and adored. After a lifetime of never quite being enough for anybody, he'd captured her heart with that one small gesture.

A simple moment. There'd been no need for flashy restaurants, diamonds, or trying to impress her with money or status. Just a quiet moment, by a river, with his arm around her, giving her a kiss.

Maddy groaned again at the memory and tried to force it back down into the recesses of her mind. *I cannot keep thinking of him in this way!* He was no longer that boy. She was no longer that girl. Time had moved on, and so had he, and it was time for her to do the same. Hadn't she come here for that very reason—a fresh start, sailing the Mediterranean, exploring the world? Pushing her own boundaries and seeking a new and different life? If she was going to do that, then she needed to find a way to deal with Nate.

If he was going to continue to be delicious and sexually attractive to her, then she needed to define new ways of dealing with him. Because she was even more broken now and he had no idea. And, if she was going to put herself back together again here, then she needed time and space to heal. She did not need to think about diving into a new relationship. What she needed to do here was focus on being confident again, being a good doctor again.

So she needed to harden her heart against Dr Nathaniel Blake. She got up and decided to go and get something to eat. Passenger clinic would be in less than an hour and she wanted to be fully fuelled before that started. And then afterwards she would come back to her cabin, maybe read some more of that self-help book she'd bought, and then get some sleep. Keeping her life simple meant keeping away from the distractions.

And Nate was the biggest distraction of them all.

'Good morning.' Nate handed some paperwork to Sylvia as Maddy arrived at the medical centre. 'Sleep well?' He wanted to extend the hand of friendship after her disappearance yesterday, show her that he didn't mind her having absconded from the sail-away party, because hey, he could hardly have a go at her for that, could he? He'd disappeared on her once, without a word. Comparatively, they were hardly the same thing, but…he didn't want there to be any hard feelings.

'No, not really. I always find it difficult to sleep in a brand-new place.'

Of course. He'd forgotten that. The first time she'd ever stayed over at his digs, he'd woken in the morning to see her just lying there, staring at the ceiling, having waited for him to wake up so they could go into work together. It was a hangover from her childhood. She'd been an orphan, raised in the care system and sent to so many different child-care centres and foster homes.

'Well, I hope you're okay to work, because we've actually got a call-out—a passenger whose family are concerned about her. I thought we could go together and you could take point; what do you think?'

She seemed to brighten and then nodded. 'Perfect. Who's the patient?'

'Seventy-nine-year-old female, travelling

with her son and daughter-in-law. She's been unable to get out of bed this morning.'

'Right. Okay. Do we take anything with us if we go to a patient's cabin?'

'We have a go bag with basics. I should have shown it to you yesterday; apologies.'

She nodded. 'Which deck?'

'Deck ten. Room 1035.'

'Let's go.'

As they headed for the lifts, Nate fell into step beside her. 'I'm sorry about yesterday, if I made you feel uncomfortable, asking you to dance.'

The lift pinged open and they stepped inside, Maddy jabbing at the button for deck ten. 'I don't dance.'

'Oh, I don't know. I think I remember you dancing with me once. New Year's Eve?'

He'd known her about a year and they'd gone to a New Year's Eve rooftop party in the heart of London. It had been freezing cold! The wind had whipped around them that high up in the city as they'd partied hard. He remembered her wearing this shimmering silver dress that skimmed the tops of her thighs, revealing her delicious legs. And all he'd been able to think about all night was how he wanted to trail his fingers up and down her thighs, find the swell of her bottom and pull her against him. But she'd been determined to dance, champagne glass in one hand, her long red hair free about her pale creamy shoulders. She'd laughed so much that night that she'd been like a wild thing, letting loose after a long and difficult day.

Maddy had wanted to stay in and not go out, but he'd persuaded her that, if they were to survive their job, then they needed to be able to disconnect from the trauma and not take it home. That New Year's Eve had been a time for fresh starts and celebration. She'd looked up at him, nodded, pulled him into her arms and whispered, 'Thank you,' into his ear. She'd felt so good in his arms that he'd taken her in that moment, in a frantic, passionate moment to celebrate life. Celebrate that they were alive.

Afterwards, they'd showered and dressed for the party and, though there'd been many beautiful women at it, his eyes had only been for her and the way that she'd danced: free, as if no-one was watching.

Only, he had been.

'That was a long time ago and under different circumstances,' she answered sharply.

'Yes, but you do, in fact, dance.' He kept his own tone light.

They emerged on deck ten and followed the numbered signs to find cabin 1035, and Maddy rapped her knuckles against the door.

It was opened by a woman in her late forties, maybe early fifties.

'You called for a medical consultation?'

'Oh, yes! Do come on in, she's over here, still in bed.'

'Thanks. I'm Dr Finch and this is Dr Blake.'

The woman nodded, then turned to the older woman in the bed. 'Peggy? The doctors are here.'

Nate stood at the end of Peggy's bed, as Maddy took point, as he'd suggested earlier.

'Hi, Peggy. I hear you're not feeling very well; can you tell me what's been happening with you?'

Peggy looked pale and weak. When she didn't speak, her son, standing next to Nate, spoke up. 'She's been a little confused lately, but we just put that down to her age, you know? She hasn't been sleeping well, and she's been slowing down a bit, but we thought it was tiredness and figured this cruise would do her some good—rest, relaxation, a bit of sea air. But she took to her bed last night, saying she felt a little nauseous, and we just assumed it was a bit of sea sickness. She's never sailed before, but when she couldn't get out of bed this morning, we got worried.'

Maddy nodded and opened her bag to get out a few things. She turned to the patient. 'Peggy,

I'm going to take some basic observations, if that's okay? I'm going to check your temperature and blood pressure; is that alright?'

Peggy nodded and Maddy placed the oxygen saturations monitor on Peggy's finger, whilst she used the aural thermometer to take her temperature. 'Slight fever. Heart rate ninety-four. Let's take your BP.' The cuff took a moment to inflate and then it deflated and the machine beeped its result. 'Ninety-six over fifty-five. Can I do a brief examination, Peggy?'

Peggy nodded again.

Nate watched carefully as Maddy performed a primary survey of the older woman, examining her head to toe and palpating her abdomen. Peggy seemed tender there.

'Right then, Peggy, your respiratory rate is twenty-three and you're showing signs of dehydration and, with your slight fever, the confusion, the weakness and the tenderness you're showing in your abdomen, I'm thinking that this is most probably a urinary tract infection. Are you eating and drinking normally?' Maddy asked.

'Not really, no.'

Maddy turned to face Nate. 'I think we should perform a urinalysis, give IV fluids to counteract her dehydration and prescribe antibiotics.' She seemed happy with her diagnosis and smiled at him, as if expecting him to agree. He could tell that she was trying to show him that she was capable.

However, there were some things that she had missed in her eagerness to impress. Normally, he would say if it sounds like hoofbeats, think horses, not zebras, and confusion and weakness in an elderly female was very often a UTI, but one couldn't assume. The urinalysis was a good test to perform, but there were one or two questions she'd left out. 'Peggy are you on any other medications?'

'I take some tablets but I don't know what they are.'

He saw Maddy realise that she'd not asked the question and knew she'd be beating herself up inside.

'She's on digoxin for her atrial fibrillation,' the younger woman said. Atrial fibrillation was a condition with which the heart's upper chambers, the atria, could beat rapidly or irregularly. Digoxin helped stabilize the heartbeat and make it stronger.

'Anything else?'

'Erm… Eric, what was she given for the swelling in her legs?'

Eric rummaged in his mother's toiletries bag and pulled out medication, turning it to read it. 'Furosemide.'

Furosemide was a diuretic. He looked towards Maddy. 'Peggy, we'd like to do a tracing of your heart. Would that be okay?'

The older woman shrugged. She was tired.

Maddy blushed as she set up the machine. He knew she was kicking herself for not asking about the recent meds, but he would salve her conscience later. Right now, they had a patient to care for. With the leads attached, the machine ran a trace and it was clear that Peggy's heart was beating slower and there was some PR elongation, revealing that it was taking longer than normal for the electrical impulses to travel from her atria to the lower chambers of her heart, the ventricles.

It was now time for Nate to take charge of this case. 'Okay, I think it's best that we take your mum into our medical bay for monitoring, IV fluids and urinalysis, as Dr Finch suggested, and blood tests. I'm hoping that this is a simple UTI, as my colleague suspected, but because of the digoxin I also just want to check to make sure her levels aren't elevated. I'll send some nurses up with a chair to bring your mother to sick bay. Is that alright?'

Eric and his wife nodded. 'Of course. Whatever you think is right.'

'Someone should be up within half an hour. You're welcome to come down with Peggy, if you wish; there's a seating area where you can wait whilst we get her settled.'

'Thank you.'

Out in the corridor on their way to the lifts, Maddy swore. 'I can't believe I missed asking about recent meds!'

'Maddy—'

'I'm so embarrassed! Patient history is key! I can't believe I did that; I'm so sorry. Honestly, I'm a much better doctor than that, it's just that I…'

He stopped her and placed his hand on her arm. 'Maddy, considering her symptoms, it was easy to assume that she has a UTI. She may very well have one! But we must make sure we ask the right questions on a cruise ship. We're *isolated* at sea, and we don't have the support of an entire hospital to back us up, so we must absolutely pinpoint our diagnoses.'

She nodded. 'Understood. I'm sorry. I promise you, I'm a much better doctor that that. I was just…nervous.'

'Why?' He didn't understand why she was nervous. She'd been a doctor for years.

Maddy looked at him uncertainly, as if she had something to say, but didn't know whether to say it. 'I had some time away recently. Took some time for myself. Coming here, returning to the job after a break, I… What with yesterday's patient that you needed to help me with, and then you saying we'd come to see this patient together, I thought you were *judging* me and I wanted to impress. And we were in that room, with everyone looking on… I thought it was an easy diagnosis and I jumped on it, without being thorough.'

She sounded so dejected, so disappointed in herself. He didn't want her to feel that way. And it was his job to support her here and help her find her confidence again after a break from medicine. 'When Peggy gets to the medical bay, what tests do you think you should run?'

She sighed. 'Check for elevated digoxin levels, urinalysis, give IV fluids for rehydration, but also check her potassium levels and renal function.'

He smiled. 'You see? You do know what to do. You just needed the breathing space. When Peggy gets to the medical bay, you're in charge of her case. You can update me as and when you get results.'

'You're putting *me* in charge? After that display?'

'Yes. Because I know you can do it and you had a blip.'

'Doctors shouldn't have blips.'

He looked down at her. 'But they do. Because they're human. Come on, let's get back. We can discuss semantics another time. We've lots to do and other patients to see.'

Peggy was diagnosed with digoxin toxicity, aggravated by dehydration from her diuretic. But, as she was now stable, the digoxin and furosemide had been stopped and she was being supported, there was no need to airlift her from the ship. Maddy had ordered continuous cardiac monitoring, IV fluids and repeat bloods in the morning to recheck digoxin levels, but there were no signs of heart arrhythmias or any further confusion and, with the fluids on board, Peggy was beginning to seem brighter.

Maddy was happy that things were looking good, but she still felt bad for having missed an obvious question in her patient history, and even more embarrassed at having done so in front of Nate.

He could have called her out. He could have berated her or written her up, but he hadn't. He'd been kind, empathetic. And he'd used it as a teaching moment. But twice now he had come to her rescue, and that was really annoying, because she'd wanted to come here and stand on her own two feet. To go and make a silly mistake like that, after years of practice, when she'd wanted to show him what she could do… *Stupid.* Luckily, it wasn't a mistake that had proved fatal. But it had been in front of Nate and God only knew what he thought of her privately.

Even though Peggy was getting better, she could feel her anxiety rising. As she sat at a terminal updating Peggy's notes, a young guy walked in. He was handsome. dark-haired like Nate, but this guy wore his hair a little longer and was clean-shaven.

'Hi. Nate around?'

'He's with a patient. Can I help? I'm a doctor, if you need medical assistance.'

'I'm good. Healthy as a horse, as far as I know. I just wanted a quick word with Nate.'

'I can take a message.'

'Okay. Can you tell him we're going to be dining in the Orchard tonight? We've got a table booked for eight p.m.'

'Okay. And your name?'

'Lucas.' The man smiled, seeming to expect her to know who he was, but she didn't. She had no idea. Was he crew? A passenger? An old friend? A new one? Maddy must have looked blank enough for him to fill the silence and explain.

'I'm his younger brother.'

Maddy blinked in surprise. 'I didn't know Nate had a brother.'

'Well, here I am, and he does. And you tell

him he'd better be there, if he wants Carlos and us to celebrate properly.'

'Who's Carlos?' she asked, confused.

'My fiancé.' Lucas presented his left hand to reveal an engagement ring, a solid-gold band inset with a diamond. 'This is the only night of the cruise in which we've both got the same night off.'

'You're crew? What do you do?'

'I'm an ice-dancer. Carlos is an acrobat in the circus show.'

Maddy had a vague idea of what Lucas was talking about. She'd browsed the ship's itinerary in her cabin last night before bed. 'Oh. Okay. Well, I'll let him know.'

'You know, it's typical of him not to mention he has family. But I suppose I can excuse him, because there were all those family issues, but…we're good now, so… Anyway, listen to me, talking like there's no tomorrow! Good to meet you, Dr…er…?'

'Finch. Madeline Finch.' She shook his hand, still surprised at this development. Nate was clearly a dark horse. Why hadn't he mentioned his brother before when they'd been junior doctors? She'd asked him once if he had any siblings—she knew she had! But he'd mumbled something about not having any, and she'd wondered if he'd been in care too, but he had said no. But now it turned out he had a brother. Why would he have kept his brother secret?

'Nice to meet you, Madeline Finch.' Lucas looked her up and down and smiled. 'You know, if he doesn't have someone to bring and he wants to bring a plus one, you'd be more than welcome.'

'Oh! You're very kind, but we're not that close,' she said, blushing, thinking about just how close she had been with Nate. There wasn't a single inch of skin on his body with which she hadn't been intimately familiar. She knew he had a birthmark on the sole of his foot. She knew he had a small circular scar on his right butt cheek from when he'd had chicken pox as a child. And she knew all about the tattoo just below his right pectoral muscle. The staff of Asclepius: a serpent-entwined rod, wielded by the Greek god Asclepius, which symbolised healing and medicine. Maybe he had more now.

But why had Nate never introduced her to his brother?

Because I wasn't important. Or a real girlfriend. I was just a warm body he needed when he wanted to rid himself of the difficulties of our days.

Had she made it too easy for him before? Had she been so willing for any form of affection, she had taken whatever he'd chosen to dole out?

'Plus this sounds like a family thing, and I'm not family,' she said.

Lucas raised a solitary eyebrow. 'Oh, puh-lease! I've sat around listening to my brother give the whole "we're a family" speech when he talks about every new team on board.'

'Does he?' Maddy smiled, amused.

'Of course! He really gets into character. Sometimes I play the role of naughty nurse just to try and derail him, but I'll give my brother credit where it's due: he can maintain focus like nobody can. I mean, you must have noticed that, right?'

She nodded. She liked Lucas. He seemed fun, easy to talk to.

'You single?' Lucas asked.

Maddy laughed. 'I'm not prepared to answer that.'

'Hah! That means you are—you just don't want to admit it. So, you're single, he's single, you're both adults and you seem like you'd be his type—gorgeous, intelligent, redhead…' Lucas leaned in and whispered, 'I shouldn't tell you this, because if he ever found out he'd be mortified, but he once told me he knew a redhead *very well indeed*, if you catch my drift?' Lucas raised both eyebrows and waggled them suggestively.

She could feel herself blushing. Lucas obviously had no idea that she was probably the redhead in question!

'Anyhoo… Do pop along this evening. If you're free, of course.'

'I'm on call,' she lied. 'But I'll pass on your message.'

'You're a star. Mwah!' He blew her a kiss and sashayed away.

She watched him go and disappear round a corner, just as the patient Nate had been with came out of his consulting room. Nate and the passenger shook hands and then he came over to stand by Maddy at the console. 'Everything okay?'

'Yes. Absolutely. I have a message for you.'

'Oh. Who from?'

She smiled. 'Your brother. Lucas.'

Now it was his turn to blush.

CHAPTER FOUR

'CARLOS! CONGRATULATIONS! SO you're finally going to make an honest man of my brother?' Nate gave him a big hug. Carlos was Spanish, with thick dark hair and twinkling eyes.

Carlos glanced at Lucas and laughed. 'As honest as I can, though to be truthful with you, I'm not sure it's doable.'

Nate smiled. 'You know him well.'

Carlos reached for Lucas's hand and squeezed it in his own. 'Well enough to put a ring on his finger. He makes me happy. Happier than I've ever been.'

Nate was pleased. It was amazing to see Lucas happy and settled with someone who loved him. He was pleased that he had found someone to be in his life. If it went well, then maybe Nate could go off and do his own thing. Not that he hadn't loved being there for his brother, and getting to know him again after all those years apart, but he'd seen him at rock bottom. Nate had vowed not to leave his side, until he saw Lucas at the peak of happiness. It was a sacrifice he'd been willing to make, and sitting here now, seeing his little brother in love, engaged to be married, well…it made his own heart sing.

Not that he could say his brother was completely out of the woods yet. Relationships were tricky things and they could go wrong any time. No, he would stay until he'd seen Lucas walk down the aisle and say 'I do'. And God forbid Carlos ever broke his heart… 'Have you named the day?'

Lucas glanced at Carlos and smiled. 'We're going to get married on board! We've asked the captain to officiate, and he's said yes, and then we'll have a second official ceremony in Spain so Carlos's family can be there.'

'Wow. So soon?'

Nate listened as Carlos expounded on his vast network of siblings, cousins, aunts, uncles, nephews and nieces. It was confusing at times, trying to remember all their names, but it was nice just to sit there and hear Carlos tell funny stories about them all, hear about how stable an upbringing Carlos had had and how close they all were, how supportive. And how this huge Spanish family was about to become his brother's.

It was what Lucas needed—stability, love,

warmth. He would be welcomed into Carlos's family with a warm embrace and it would make Nate feel easier about branching away to follow his own dreams that he'd put on hold for his brother.

'Are you happy for me, Nate?' asked Lucas.

'Of course I am! You've found the love of your life.' He smiled and sipped his drink.

'Now we just need you to find yours and we'll both be happy.'

'I am happy.'

Lucas leaned in. 'You think I don't realise that you pressed pause on your own life so that I could find my feet in mine?'

'I've not pressed pause.'

'No? Why have you not come to dinner tonight with someone? A ship full of beauties and you sit here alone!'

'A ship full of potential patients, Lucas! I can't date them.'

'You could date that pretty doctor in your clinic—the redhead, Dr Finch! She's gorgeous! And I know you have a thing for redheads!'

Nate sipped his wine. He'd made the mistake of once telling Lucas about Madeline. But not by name, so his brother had no idea that the much-missed redhead he'd left behind in London was the very same person he was suggesting should have joined them for dinner.

They'd been sitting together one night in Nate's flat. It had been Lucas's first night out of rehab. He'd been clean, sober for the first time in years, and they'd been telling each other about the missed chances in their life. The missed chances when they both could have had something big.

Lucas had mentioned the day he had come out to their parents, so sure that they would be happy for him, so certain that there would be happy tears and hugs, and that they would embrace him and tell him that they loved him. They'd always adored him—he'd had no reason to suspect any other reaction. But it hadn't happened that way. His dad had kicked off, their mother had gone silent in shock and, in the middle of a raging row with his father, Lucas had run out of the house, heartbroken, his dreams in tatters, his very identity, who he was, dragged through the mud.

His father had accused him of causing them shame and embarrassment, saying that he would not have *someone like that* in the house, when *someone like that* had made them so proud with his GCSE results. The *someone like that* who had impressed them so much when he'd starred in his school's production of *Frankenstein*. The *someone like that* who had captained his cricket team and took them to victory for the first time in the school's history.

'They liked me enough when I followed their path, but couldn't love me enough when I found my own,' he'd said.

Lucas had begun to live on the streets and got in with the wrong people, turned to drugs.

'A different reaction from them and my future might have been different. They might still be alive.'

They'd both sat in silence that night, no words needed. Nate had learned that his parents' drinking had got much worse after he'd left. They'd gone out in their car and his father Bill had caused a car accident that killed them both instantly.

And Lucas had wrongly carried the guilt of their deaths into rehab, until Nate had come back into his life and put him right. He'd told him he wasn't to blame. That it wasn't his fault. That their parents had been flawed, that they were all flawed. That everyone made mistakes. And then he'd then listed his—including walking away from a redhead…

Lucas could never know she was on this ship. Because if he knew he would not stop until he tried to get them back together. Which was a terrible idea.

'I can't date a colleague,' he said, trying to derail that line of conversation.

'Why on earth not? She's your type! Are you telling me you're going to be celibate for the entire contract?'

'Can we talk about something else?' he asked, feeling uncomfortable.

'Leave your brother alone,' Carlos said, placing his hand on Lucas's.

'Thank you, Carlos. See? He's on my side.' Nate smiled and they clinked glasses.

'Hmm,' Lucas said, trying to sound annoyed and failing.

The rest of the evening went very well and Nate discovered a lot about Carlos that he liked. He was the right man for Lucas. He knew about his brother's struggles with drugs and accepted him for who he was, which was all that Lucas had ever looked for.

Nate often felt guilty about not having been there during those turbulent years after Lucas had come out. If he had not abandoned his brother to save himself, then maybe everything would have turned out differently. But he'd had to leave. He couldn't wait to escape.

His stepdad, Lucas's father, had made it clear that he'd never liked Nate, being the son of his wife's first husband, who'd passed. They'd never warmed to one another and, though Nate had initially been thrilled at the idea of having a younger brother, it had quickly become clear that Nate was second best. Even his own mum, to keep the peace, had often sided with her new husband and, feeling unloved and unwanted, feeling a burden, Nate had left, tearing apart the two brothers.

He'd hated leaving Lucas behind. He loved him and, when Lucas had fallen off the radar, he'd just assumed that his stepfather had poisoned Lucas against him, not realising that Lucas had already turned to drugs and was lost in a world of pain.

So much hurt and destruction, all because one man—his stepfather—had come into their lives like a grenade, blowing them apart in all directions, broken, bleeding and forever maimed.

'Let me raise a glass…to Lucas and Carlos. Congratulations on your engagement and may you have a happy lifetime ahead of you both.'

Maddy had come up to look at the stars. There was an observation deck at the top of the ship, with a room that had star charts decorating the walls and ceilings and a selection of telescopes bolted to the floor.

She'd never been to sea before. She'd never really been out of urban areas, really, and she'd heard someone say once that, the further away from light pollution, the clearer the stars. Tonight was such a clear night and the skies were inky black. As she wanted to explore the ship, as well as open herself up to new experiences, stargazing had seemed the perfect choice.

I might like it!

It would be looking at something bigger than herself. She imagined each star as a sun, millions of miles away in a vast galaxy; imagined looking at constellations, maybe other planets! She'd perused the beginner guides in the room and, as the ship cruised through the darkness of the mouth of the Bay of Biscay, Maddy gazed up at the skies and allowed herself to imagine other worlds, other galaxies.

It made her own situation, her own difficulties, seem insignificant. What did it matter that she was sharing a ship and a medical bay with Nate? She ought to be grateful she'd become reacquainted with an old friend! What did it matter that he'd left without a word? That wasn't *her* fault! That was *his*.

The stars were beautiful. Life was beautiful. Here she was, forging a new path, finding new possibilities. She was going to travel the world as a cruise-ship doctor and she'd told herself that, if this contract went well, then would travel the entire world before she stopped and returned to England. Why not? She had no-one waiting for her at home. Why not lead a different life, full of exploration?

The stars seemed to twinkle acknowledgement at her. *Good idea*, they seemed to say. Peaceful, soothed, she headed back down into the ship and towards the lift that would take her down to her deck. She passed a row of restaurants and saw couples through the window, smiling at one another, in love, one couple holding hands. She was happy for them and did not envy them their happiness. She would find joy in other things. Someone was being surprised with a birthday cake adorned with a firework fizzing and sparking away as their family launched into a rendition of *Happy Birthday*.

She briefly thought of her own past birthdays, in care homes. The other kids would gather around and it had been okay. She'd made peace with her childhood. Lately, her birthdays had been spent with colleagues and friends, but no-one important in her life. Afterwards, she'd always bought a beautiful cupcake for herself, put a candle on it, blown it out and made a wish. She missed her old colleagues—Jordan, Imran and Kelly.

She saw groups chatting and laughing, everyone having a good time in each other's company, and felt alone. She hoped that Nate was enjoying his evening with his brother and new fiancé. That he was happy, raising a glass to celebrate the engagement. As she turned the corner that would take her down to the crew area, she bumped into someone coming in the other direction.

'Oh! I'm sorry, I...'

It was as if thinking about him had conjured him, like magic.

Nate. Looking devastatingly handsome in a dinner jacket and open-necked white shirt, a hint of tanned skin below.

'Sorry, I didn't mean to bump into you. I must pay more attention where I'm going,' he said, cheeks flushed, eyes sparkling as his gaze raked over her.

She'd not put on anything special. She'd just wanted to be comfortable, even though it was formal night on the ship and most people were dressed up to the nines. Maddy reckoned she probably stuck out like a sore thumb in her grey jogging bottoms, trainers and over-sized top but, after a day of being dressed smartly and attending crew and passengers, it had felt good just to kick back and wear something comfortable. 'No, no, *I* wasn't looking where I was going,' she apologised, stepping back from him, taking herself out of the danger zone.

Because, the second she'd bumped into him, her body had fizzed into life. First of all, he smelt *good.* And not the kind of good that was something simply having a pleasing aroma, such as recently cut grass or freshly brewed coffee, but the kind of good that drove her senses wild. That made her want to step into his personal space and breathe him in some more. The kind of good that urged her to rip open his shirt, sending buttons flying, place a hand upon his flesh and her cheek to his pecs and just *enjoy.* To trail her finger down his chest and over his smooth skin and slip that shirt from his broad shoulders and trail kisses over his body…

Secondly, he *looked* amazing, casually cool, as if the suit had been made just for him. It draped his body just so, hugging it perfectly, emphasising his neat waist and fit body, as if he was born to model this suit in particular. The dark jacket brought out the honeyed hazel in his eyes, the white shirt giving him a healthy glow.

And thirdly, in the moment she'd bumped into him, her hand had gone to his chest and she'd felt the solidity of him, the hardness of him. All together, her mind had gone into overload and had provided her with many flashbacks of many nights spent with this man and what he could do to her. What he had done to her and how he had made her feel. And that had been years ago! What could he do now? The possibilities were endless and, though she yearned to find out, she knew she had to hold herself back from him and protect herself, because this man could so easily take her heart again and crush it beneath his perfectly polished shoes, like he had done once before.

The memory that he had abandoned her, without explanation and without apology, was like a bucket of ice water dashed over her head: stark, bewildering and utterly sobering.

'Have you been out to dinner?' she asked, her brain reaching for something safe to ask, even though she knew the answer, having delivered his brother's invitation herself.

'Yes, at the Orchard,' he replied, nodding, seemingly happy to stick with safe topics too.

Had he had as much of a visceral reaction to her as she had had to him?

Probably not.

She was only in a jogging outfit that hid her body. Her hair was up in a messy topknot, and she'd no make-up on, and no perfume. *He probably thinks I look like a slob. Probably thinks he had a lucky escape!*

A twinge of annoyance washed over her. Why couldn't she have looked amazing? Why hadn't she put on her best party outfit and gone dancing down in the crew entertainment area with her hair done, her make-up completed to perfection, wearing a dress that pulled her in, in all the right places, hugging her body and emphasising her curves, showing legs up to there and a cleavage that drew the eye?

Actually, I don't think I've ever dressed like that in my entire life.

'With your brother. Lucas, right?'

He nodded. 'And his fiancé.'

'Carlos, if I remember. Did it go well?'

'Absolutely! Lucas has found himself a great guy…someone who balances him perfectly. Provides the sense to his crazy…'

He was looking her up and down, taking in her grey jogging outfit.

She felt herself blush. 'Sounds like he's found the right one. He's lucky. Not many people get that.'

'No.'

Was he getting closer? It felt as though he was.

She could feel her heart pounding in her chest. 'Those sorts of people are hard to find…' she said, her words faltering as Nate stepped even closer.

Was he drunk? Or were his eyes glazed because of something else…such as lust?

She'd succumbed to that look so many times before, unable and completely unwilling to protest, because she'd wanted him so much too. And it had felt good to be wanted, even if it had just been for her body and nothing else. Just to be seen, noticed, wanted… It had been enough for someone starved of affection and attention.

It felt for a moment as if they were back at London Saint and Nate had found them a corner to be in, to share a moment: a touch, a brush of lips, something to sate them both.

She was up against a wall now and he was so close. As she gazed at his face, she tried to not let herself be hypnotised by the beauty of it: the soft swell and fullness of his lips, the sharp slice of his jaw, the delicate curve to his cheekbones. Those eyes that she'd so often stared into as they'd had sex, watching the ways his pupils dilated and grew darker, larger; the way his hair fell about his face… 'Nate, we…'

She didn't get to say anything else, for suddenly he was kissing her. Those lips melted against hers, his body squashing her against the wall, his hard body grinding into her. A low moan came to her throat as she whimpered in surrender and felt utter unfettered joy at being kissed by him again.

How long had she spent mourning the loss of his touch? How long had she grieved, thinking she would never see him again? Those first few weeks of him being gone had been awful. She'd felt as if she'd lost everything: her colleague, her best friend…her lover. He'd been the one person who saw her, who got her, who understood her. She had loved him so much, but had been so afraid to tell him, and he'd had no idea what it had done to her when he had just upped and left. And still she *did not know why.*

Maddy knew she ought to do the sensible thing and pull away, not allow herself to be dragged back into his web, to be swept away by his kiss, but it was Nate! He was kissing her again; how many times had she lain in her bed after he'd left, praying to a god she wasn't sure that she believed in that, if she could have just one more kiss, just one more moment with him, then she would be satisfied. That it would be enough.

And so selfishly, not knowing if she would get this chance again, she pushed aside her anger, her pain, her grief and her *questions* and simply kissed him back with everything that she had.

It was like time travel, like going at hyper-speed, like going in slow motion. It was fire-works and electricity. It was her oxygen, her light and dark. She could feel herself being pulled in all directions as his kiss deepened. And the *heat* of it…she couldn't breathe, she couldn't think. She just knew that she *wanted*: wanted more.

His body was against hers, his arousal pressed

up against her. She knew without a shadow of a doubt that, if they'd been back in her cabin and not in a public corridor, she would have been ripping his clothes off him by now and dragging him into her bed, where she'd be able to consume every single inch of him.

Sod the past, sod the pain, sod being abandoned! 'Nate...' she breathed as his lips trailed down her neck and then back up, reclaiming her mouth, his hands in her hair, as if he couldn't touch enough of her. She soaked up every sensation, trying to commit them to memory so she could enjoy them again later. His thumb ran over her bottom lip and she grabbed at his hand with her own and licked it.

Nate groaned and his eyes met hers and suddenly, somehow, the spell was broken. He stepped back, away from her, dishevelled from their contact, his gaze glassy, and he was frowning.

She stepped forward, still needing more, not sure why he'd ended it, why he'd stepped away. She was stunned, her body in a state of fission.

'I'm sorry, Mads, that was a...mistake. We should never have...' He blinked, shook his head. '*I* should never have... I've had too much to drink, I... I'm sorry.' He looked down and away, and headed away from her without another word, leaving her breathless and confused.

She watched him depart, mouth agape, left wanting, left by him *yet again*!

How many times am I going to let him do this to me?

Disgusted with herself, ashamed, she wiped her mouth on her sleeve, pulled up her hood and headed in the opposite direction.

Nate woke with a stinking hangover and groaned. How had this happened? Dinner with Lucas and Carlos. His brother stuck to mocktails during dinner, and Nate had joined him to support him. But then, as the night had worn on, someone had encouraged them to have something stronger. *We should celebrate properly.* Champagne had been ordered. Corks had popped to toast the happy couple. They'd ordered a bottle and, judging by his headache, the way his body felt and the taste in his mouth, Nate feared he had drunk the entire thing!

Ugh.

Standing, he made his way to the *en suite* and switched on the light, wincing at its brightness and his stark reflection in the mirror. He needed a shower; he needed to freshen up to look less like a zombie and feel more like a human being.

Turning on the water, he stripped himself of his clothes, feeling that he was missing something important, but he couldn't think what it might be. He soaped himself down and washed his hair, and was rinsing out the shampoo when a stark and vivid image came into his mind: kissing Maddy.

Wait...

He forced the recall into full Technicolor vision. He'd bumped into her. They'd collided in the corridor. Carlos and Lucas had already left and gone to their cabin, as their room was in a different direction from his. Nate had just been to the bathroom and come round the corner, and then there she was, looking beautiful and effortlessly gorgeous in jogging bottoms and an over-sized top with a hood. She'd looked so warm and cosy...inviting!

His gaze had fallen to her mouth as she'd said something...what had she said? He wasn't sure about that part, but what he did remember was watching her lips move: full, soft, pink lips. Lips that he remembered had once trailed down his body, bringing with them delight and ecstasy, and he wasn't sure what had happened in his brain then. He'd spent the entire evening watching Carlos and Lucas so happy and in love and he'd envied his brother having someone. Of course Lucas deserved happiness after all he had been through, and Nate craved the same, but everyone on this boat was a potential patient. He could hardly go dancing, end up kissing someone in a darkened corner and have a one-night stand, not when that wasn't what he was looking for.

I wanted what Lucas has. Someone I knew. Someone I had a long history with. Someone I felt comfortable with. Someone who I had deep feelings for.

And there she was, in all her natural, beautiful glory—like a gift! And he'd succumbed to his desires in that moment without thinking it through. For a moment there, he'd been utterly lost in how she'd made him feel that he'd forgotten to think with his brain…though, to be fair, that part of his body hadn't had possession of the blood flow right there and then.

Suddenly he'd been right where he was meant to be.

Kissing Maddy had felt so right, feeding his soul and his senses in a way they'd long forgotten. For too long he had felt like a neglected and unloved plant in the middle of an arid desert, and Maddy had been the rain, dropping refreshing water onto thirsty leaves and into his roots. All he'd wanted to do was drink her up, drink every drop she had to give; take everything.

And then…reality and logic had crept into his brain, reminding him that he wasn't good for her, and he'd stepped back, suddenly aware that he had stepped over a line. Stepped over a boundary that he should never have crossed. Maddy was his past, and he'd made a promise to himself that he would never go back there. Besides, he wasn't sure she deserved to get involved with him again. He'd abandoned her, left just as things had been starting to get complicated in his mind, and she deserved more than he could give. He was selfish. He left when things got tough, and she'd been deserted enough in life without him adding to it even more.

Besides, she probably wasn't even single any more…even if she had kissed him back.

And now he would have to face her at work.

I'll apologise again—clear the air—then everything will be fine.

By the time he reached the medical bay that morning, the two painkillers he'd taken were just starting to tackle the champagne headache, and the water he'd chugged was sloshing around unpleasantly in his stomach, but he forced a smile for the staff. He asked Sylvia to send Maddy through to his office when she arrived.

There was a knock on his door five minutes later and he looked up to see her standing there, a vision in blue scrubs. He felt his body respond at seeing her again and he had to fight down the urge to rush over to her, close his office door, let down her hair from its clip and kiss her until his lips got sore and he needed to breathe.

'Ah, yes, Maddy. Come in, close the door.'

She raised an eyebrow. 'I think it's best that we leave the door open, don't you?'

Of course. He nodded. 'Then at least take a seat.' The words 'I won't bite,' were on the tip of his tongue and he had to count to ten until the urge to say them was gone. Unfortunately, the image of him *actually* biting her was very distracting.

Maddy settled herself into the chair furthest from him.

'I would like to formally apologise for my behaviour last night towards you. It was inappropriate and you caught me in a low moment.' He sighed. 'Sorry, I don't mean to try to excuse my behaviour. You are welcome to file a formal complaint, if you wish.'

Maddy frowned and shook her head. 'I don't think that's necessary. We all make mistakes.'

He let out a breath, relief flooding him. That she might have taken this further was not out of the question; he'd have hated, yet accepted, the black mark against his name. Clearly their friendship and previous relationship had saved him from that. 'So, you're happy for us to continue on as colleagues?'

She met his gaze sharply at his last word. ‘Yes. That’s all we ever can be.’

The feel of her pressed up against the wall, her soft body melting into his, flashed back into his mind like a torment. ‘Of course.’

Emily Simons came into the medical bay with her mother. It turned out the cruise was a kind of celebratory holiday they were sharing together, as Emily had finished her exams. Unfortunately for the sixteen-year-old, she’d been up all night with gastrointestinal pain and now she was feeling sick and couldn’t stomach the idea of food.

‘What time did this start?’ Maddy asked the young girl.

‘About ten o’ clock last night. We’d had a celebratory meal at the Sakura Japanese restaurant, and then gone on to the circus show, but we went back to our cabin early because I didn’t feel great.’

‘Eat anything new or strange at the restaurant?’

‘I tried oysters for the first time.’

Maddy smiled. ‘What did you think?’

‘Yucky on the way down *and* on the way back up.’

‘You’ve been vomiting?’

‘No, but the burps I’ve had feel like I might.’

'Okay. Any episodes of diarrhoea?'

'No, just pain.'

'Since ten o' clock last night?'

Emily nodded.

Maddy was writing everything down on a piece of paper, gathering her thoughts. 'And do you have any medical issues I ought to know about?'

'No.'

Maddy looked to Emily's mum for confirmation, but she seemed to agree. 'Any medications that you usually take or have had recently prescribed?' There was no way she was going to forget *that* question again. She couldn't afford to mess up, not after all that had happened with Nate. That mess up with Peggy—who was already feeling much better, thankfully—and then the kiss…

That kiss…she felt so stupid for letting it happen! To allow him to get inside her walls once more. So much for fresh starts. All she'd managed to do was repeat the past mistakes. She would not embarrass herself again and they would remain strictly professional.

'No, nothing.'

'Alright. Well, I'm going to need to check you over—perform some obs such as your temperature, your blood pressure, that kind of thing—

and have a little feel of your tummy, would that be alright?'

Emily nodded.

She smiled. 'Don't worry. We'll help get you sorted.'

The young girl's blood pressure was slightly elevated, but nothing to worry about. Probably as a result of her worry about being in the medical bay and having been up all night in tummy pain. There was no temperature, so that was good. Blood sugars were normal and, when she palpated Emily's abdomen, she found no signs of tenderness over McBurney's Point which might have indicated an appendicitis, though her patient did report tenderness directly over her stomach.

Once her patient was sitting back with her mother, Maddy gave her assessment. 'Well, I think what we have here is a mild case of gastritis. That means your stomach is inflamed, possibly aggravated by the new foods you're trying or the stress of having finished exams, maybe both. I'm going to suggest you rest, get lots of fluids, even if you don't want to eat, and I'll also prescribe you some antacids to help deal with that. If you do eat, I suggest soft, plain foods, nothing exotic, alright?' She smiled.

Emily smiled back. 'So, I'll be okay?'

'Yes. But if you start being sick, or get diarrhoea, or if you feel like it's getting worse, you come straight back and see me, okay?'

'Thank you, Dr Finch.'

'You're most welcome.'

When her patient was gone, Maddy tapped her clinical notes into the computer, noting all her observations, her reasonings, conclusion and recommendations. The more she wrote, the more confident she was in her assessment, and she pressed *save*.

She had no patients waiting, so she carried out some admin, but her mind was on last night and this morning: the kiss; Nate asking if she wanted to file a complaint. That would have been a fine start to her career on cruise ships, wouldn't it, filing a charge of sexual harassment against her boss? No, she couldn't do it. If it had been someone she hadn't known, then maybe, but she and Nate had a history and it was different. She could complain if she wanted, and she felt any woman would be well within their rights to do so if a boss had overstepped the mark like that, but she didn't want to.

She felt that she and Nate could get through it. Their friendship had always got them through anything and it had been there first, before any sexy shenanigans had ever happened between them, and she didn't want to lose that, even if he had just upped and left for years without explanation.

Speaking of which, he still hasn't told me why, or said sorry for that.

She figured she would never get an explanation. Not now. Too much water had gone under the bridge. *Too much sea under the* Serendipity, she thought, with a wry smile.

What had last night's kiss proved, anyway? That he still felt something for her? No. He'd had too much to drink, he'd said. He'd spent the evening watching a loved up couple and had felt…what?

Maybe he'd felt a little of what she'd felt for years, seeing everyone else finding someone, creating their own families. And Maddy…she was on her own, had always been on her own. And no-one had ever made her feel for them the way she'd felt for Nate. They'd not even come close and she hated the fact that she still had Nate on a pedestal, despite the fact that he had hurt her.

What did that say about her? That she was misguided? Used to being treated badly that she'd accepted it from him too? That she was so used to being overlooked that his behaviour had not been abhorrent, but just what she was used to?

You sad, sad woman. And you always get maudlin when you're hungry.

Maddy headed off to the crew's mess, grabbed herself a jacket potato and chicken salad with dressing, sat down at a table and opened up on her phone a book she was reading. It was a non-fiction title about a woman stranded on a desert island and how she'd survived. She'd just got to the part where the woman used her bra to make a pair of slippers for her bare feet when she felt someone arrive at her table. She looked up. 'Hey.'

'May I join you?' It was Nate, holding his own tray.

By rights, she ought to tell him to go away, to keep his distance. How did he expect her to sit there and eat her food, when being this close to him kept reminding her of that kiss last night? But she'd told him that there wasn't a problem and that they could work together, and what did colleagues do but have lunch together? 'Take a seat.'

He slid into the chair opposite her. 'How are you enjoying ship food?'

'It's good.' She looked down at his plate of chilli. 'You never used to like spicy food.'

He smiled wryly. 'No, I know. But when you start travelling the globe, you begin trying other cuisines, don't you?'

'I'll tell you at the end of the contract.'

He took a moment to stir his drink.

Maddy gazed at him. Just last night he'd pressed her against a wall and kissed her, and now they sat opposite one another, distanced, propriety ruling once more. 'How's your head?'

He laughed. 'It was bad first thing, but I'm feeling better now.'

She nodded. 'I should have shouted more. Maybe slammed a cupboard or two—most definitely the door on my way out.' She winked at him to show she was joking, then flushed. *What the hell am I doing?*

'I appreciate you not doing *any* of those things. I don't think my skull would have taken it. I saw your notes this morning on that teenage girl, Emily.'

'Oh yes?'

'I thought they were great. Very thorough. A solid work-up of the patient; clear differential and notes. You documented everything and your diagnosis and prognosis were exactly what I would have thought too.'

She was relieved. After her initial embarrassment at forgetting to ask Peggy about recent medications, she'd been keen to redeem herself in Nate's eyes. 'I was worried that it could be food poisoning after she mentioned she'd had oysters, but without the sickness and diarrhoea

I leaned towards gastritis and didn't want to second-guess myself.'

'And that's what I need from the doctors in my team: confidence. And you handled it well. It's smart medicine.'

She smiled at his praise. It meant a lot to her. She'd once had so much confidence leading the A&E department, confidence that had been broken and shattered into a million pieces after her attack. When she'd screwed up in front of him, she'd been appalled, so this felt good… very good. And she sensed that he was keen to give her some good feedback after his behaviour. 'Thank you.'

'You're welcome.' He smiled back at her.

She very quickly realised that she was staring into his kind eyes and losing herself a little in them. She looked away, breaking the contact. It wouldn't do to think that he had any other intention towards her other than that of being her boss, her mentor. Losing herself in his eyes could only lead to more heartache. She pushed her plate away. 'I, er, ought to go. There's a crew clinic coming up.'

'You haven't eaten your lunch.'

'No, um…' She was about to say everything was fine—she would grab something later—but there came a huge bang from the crew galley, voices shouting, plates and trays tumbling to the floor, and smoke—lots and lots of smoke.

And then the shrill sound of a fire alarm began to sound.

Nate got to the crew galley first, stepping back as some of the kitchen staff made their escape from the kitchen that was quickly filling with smoke. The air seemed thick with a smell. *Oil?* A crew member caught Nate's arms as he stumbled out, face sweating. 'I think one of the fryers went! Tried to put it out, but…' He shook his head and coughed, struggling to breathe. 'I think Manuel is still trying!'

He watched as Maddy assessed the man for any visible burns. 'Get to the medical bay! Tell them to send help!' she said.

The man nodded, coughing, and staggered away into the arms of some other crew who helped him walk away.

Nate knew that if someone was still in the kitchen, still trying to breathe in these thick fumes and smoke, then they were in real danger, not only from the fire, but from damage to their lungs and throat. He saw a towel hanging on a rack by the door and grabbed it, then rushed over to the drinks station in the mess and poured water over it, then he looked to Maddy. 'Stay here. I'm going in for Manuel.'

'Not on your own, you're not! It's dangerous. We go together!'

'I can't risk having you injured too!' he yelled, trying to be heard over the alarm. Hopefully, the maintenance and fire crew would arrive soon to assist.

'We go in together or not at all!' she insisted.

He could sense that he was not going to win this one, so he ripped the towel in two and gave her half. 'Put it over your mouth, it should help against the fumes. Stay low!'

She nodded and clutched the cloth to her face.

He could see in her eyes that she was scared, but by god, the girl had some steel balls! She was determined to go in with him, and he was most grateful for that, but also terrified that she would get hurt. If something happened to her…

His heart was hammering in his chest from fear, from worrying about her, the thick smoke, the crackle of flames he could hear in the kitchen. He could hear someone trying to use a fire extinguisher, then the sound of a clunk, as if it had been dropped to the floor. 'Manuel?' he yelled.

No answer. Overhead the sprinklers sprang into action, raining down on them and soaking everything.

'Over there!' Maddy pointed through the smoke and water. He followed her finger.

Just barely visible, they saw a shape on the floor: a cook, an extinguisher by his side.

He could feel the heat of the flames as they got closer, scurrying low across the floor, blinking back the burning smoke in their watering eyes.

They reached Manuel and Nate pressed his fingers to the man's pulse. It was there, but thready. 'We need to get him out!' he tried to yell, coughing his way through the words. Now he was glad she was there. It would take both of them to get the cook out of there. If he'd been alone, he'd have had to try and drag the man himself, and in this thick smoke, with oil on the floor. It could have been impossible. With her to help, they had some luck on their side. Thankfully, there weren't many flames, it was mostly smoke.

Shielding Manuel, they began to drag him back the way they'd come, hoping they were going in the right direction. There was another bang, another flare of light, and Nate threw himself over Manuel and Maddy, knocking her to the floor as flames flared from a pan or grill.

Maddy yelped. For a very brief moment, a millisecond maybe, time stood still. The fire alarm still blared loudly all around them, sprinklers soaked them, the smoke still billowed, the stench of oil continued to coat his nasal passages and his throat and he was very concerned as to why Manuel was out cold. Nate lay over Maddy, his body covering hers like a shield, her scared eyes looking up at him above the cloth that covered her lower face and his heart pounding like it had never pounded before.

'Are you alright?' he asked.

She stared back at him, shocked, uncertain, confused. 'Define alright.'

He felt himself smile, despite it all. Sarcasm; she was okay.

At that moment, extra crew came in to fight the blaze and oil fire dressed in fire-resistant clothes. Manuel got handed over to the other doctors who had attended after receiving the emergency call, and Nate and Maddy got to their feet and exited the galley kitchen back into the mess, where the air was most definitely cleaner, though not great.

Genevieve fussed over them, sat them both down together and began examining them.

He saw a tear in Maddy's top and a red line of blood on her shoulder. 'You're bleeding.'

Maddy looked at it blankly, then over at him. 'So are you.'

She was staring at his chin and he reached up to touch it and found warm wetness. His fingers were red. 'It's nothing.'

'You did amazing in there,' she said softly.

'So did you. I couldn't have done it without you,' he replied, meaning every word. She'd been so brave, going into the kitchen with him to rescue Manuel.

The crew's mess was filling with people—medics, other crew—and then the captain of the ship appeared. He was tall and looked pristine in his perfectly white shirt as he hurried over to them. 'Are you both alright?'

'Minor abrasions, captain. Nothing serious,' Genevieve said.

'Was anyone seriously hurt?'

'Maybe Manuel. He tried to put out the fire,' Nate said, coughing slightly.

'I'll find out. You two get to medical.'

'Aye aye, captain.' He gave a mock salute. Captain Thomas laid a reassuring and thankful hand on Nate's shoulder, smiled at Maddy and then headed over to get information from the fire teams.

'Think he'll turn the ship around?' Maddy asked.

'Depends on how bad it is.'

Genevieve applied gauze to Maddy's shoulder. 'Come on, you two. Medical bay… And no offence, Dr Blake, but I'm in charge right now, okay?'

Nate smiled. That was just fine.

CHAPTER FIVE

SHE AND NATE had got away with very minor abrasions. The kitchen staff had luckily not been close when the fryer had gone, and one man had suffered a small burn that was easily dealt with. Manuel had slipped on oil and had simply been stunned when they'd dragged him out. The fire crew had got control of the fire and thankfully, with their quick response and the sprinkler system working effectively, there'd actually been minimal damage to the galley kitchen. It had all just simply seemed a lot worse than it was due to the smoke caused by the oil in the fryer.

The passengers on board had not noticed a thing, and there was a secondary crew mess, so the captain decided to continue with the cruise and the maintenance team was busy repairing the crew galley as they sailed into Vigo. The captain had given Nate, Maddy, Manuel and the kitchen crew strict instructions to disembark and enjoy the port for the day. So that was why Maddy had Nate knocking on her cabin door that morning to escort her into town, dressed casually in a white polo shirt and navy shorts that showed off his gorgeously tanned and toned legs, to escort her into town.

'Wow. Look at you!' she said, not used to seeing Nate like this. Normally he was dressed in trousers or scrubs. Or was naked. She'd never seen him in holiday mode.

'I was about to say the same about you. That dress is beautiful!'

She'd chosen a summer dress that skimmed just above her knee. It had spaghetti straps and was white with a dark-blue pattern printed on it. Somehow they'd matched colours. She'd left her long hair loose, but it was held back with large sunglasses and, of course, she'd smothered herself with the obligatory suncream. The scratch on her shoulder from the fire was a dark line and slightly bruised, but she barely noticed it.

Somehow, strangely, she was looking forward to spending a day in Spain with Nate. The fire, and being in a dangerous situation like that, had made her feel that maybe her long-held grudge seemed petty on the face of things. Nate hadn't known the extent of her feelings. They weren't committed, so maybe she ought just to forget it.

Last night, she'd read up a little on Vigo, the

'olive city'. It was famed for its seafood, had a historic port and was a gateway to the beautiful Cies Island—a national park that boasted stunning beaches, rich birdlife and beautiful scenery, which sounded right up her alley.

Since her attack, Maddy had often sought solace in nature when she could. It was in parks, mostly, as she'd not really left the city, and she'd used a lot of meditation apps that synthesised the sounds of nature and birdsong. And, since she and Nate had just been through something traumatic, the island of Cies sounded perfect. Nate had offered to book them a place on the ferry that would take them there.

'Thank you. Ready to go?'

'As I'll ever be.' She was excited. Right now, it seemed hard to believe that she'd never travelled like this before. In the care system, there'd been a trip to the seaside booked once and Maddy had looked forward to it hugely. But on the day in question she'd not been very well, having woken with an upset stomach, and the decision had been made to leave her behind—which basically seemed to be the story of her life.

But now she was here, in the port of Vigo, and hugely excited about exploring all that it had to offer.

'As it's high season, I had to arrange official authorisation for us to go to Cies.'

'Really?'

'Yes. It's a protected area and the beach there, the Praia das Rodas, is apparently one of the most beautiful beaches in the world.'

'I can't wait!' She felt like a little girl, going on holiday for the first time. And after the stress of yesterday she needed a little relaxation. The repairs in the crew mess were coming along nicely and Manuel and the cook with a minor burn, were both doing well. 'I never, ever thought that I'd be abroad for the first time with you.'

'And I never thought that I would get to see that smile again, but…here we are.'

She glanced at him as they walked towards disembarkation. So he had thought of her after leaving, then; that was interesting—good, even! He hadn't just walked away with no regrets. He hadn't just walked away from her and forgotten her. He'd *missed* her.

Or he's just saying that to make me feel better.

She didn't want to doubt him. She didn't want anything to spoil this moment. They might not be together, but they were friends, and they'd just been through something traumatic together, so it was only right that they got to have some fun. Maddy didn't mind there being a ceasefire where her feelings were concerned so they could just forget the past and enjoy *the present.*

The sun shone down on them as they stepped off the ship and, feeling the warm rays soothe her flesh, she felt herself relax in an instant. Maddy could see palm trees, and she laughed. Palm trees were one of those things that existed in her mind as being *elsewhere*; somewhere exotic and abroad. She was used to oak, silver birch, or horse chestnut trees. Palm trees meant *holidays*, and already she could feel her happiness increasing.

Nate guided them to the ferry that would take them the forty-five-minute journey over to Cies Island. She sat nervously on her seat in the open deck and snapped pictures with her phone as they sailed across the sea towards the island.

She saw green hills and craggy cliffs, the air above the islands dotted with white gulls, and pretty soon they were sailing into a shell-shaped harbour that had beautiful white sands and clear blue waters. 'Oh my gosh…this place is *beautiful*!' She could already feel the stress leaving her and could already feel the desire to explore and enjoy this place! And, with Nate at her side, this was…well, unbelievable. If this had been before, then she would have taken his hand in hers without thinking twice.

But it wasn't before, this was *now*, and they

were both different people. And she'd told him—colleagues only.

Nate hauled his backpack onto his shoulders. 'I took the liberty of bringing a little food for us to enjoy later. Maybe a beach picnic? But first, do you want to take a walk with me up to the viewing point?'

'Sounds great.'

There seemed to be a group of new arrivals doing the same thing. A lot had gone straight down to the beach, but some were walking ahead of Maddy and Nate. She began to take a lot of pictures. 'I want to remember everything,' she said, laughing.

'Here. Let me take a picture of you over there. We'll get the beach and the cliffs as a backdrop.'

She blushed standing in front of him, tucking her hair behind her ears when a soft breeze blew it in front of her face.

He showed it to her and she couldn't stop smiling. She wasn't usually a fan of herself in pictures, and luckily there'd never been anyone around her who'd wanted to take them. But in the one Nate took, he seemed to capture something about her.

'Let's do a selfie. Join me,' she suggested, not really thinking it through when Nate pressed up close against her so they could both be within the frame capture. She felt his arm snake around her and rest on a post as he moved in close and they both smiled and laughed nervously. When she pressed the button, the picture showed a very happy couple. *Anyone who didn't know us might think we were in love.*

Maddy put her phone away for a while as they continued the walk. It had boardwalk in places, but was mostly a stone, uphill path that weaved its way through rocks and trees until they finally reached the viewing point over an hour later. She was hot and tired, yet exhilarated when she saw the view of the rolling green cliffs, the crystal-blue waters, the curved slice of white sandy beach. And beyond the sea, the port of Vigo and *Serendipity* moored within it. Spain lay beyond it, all rippling in the heat of the day. 'I don't think I've ever seen anything so beautiful in all of my life!' she said.

'I know what you mean.'

She thought he was agreeing with her about the view, but when she turned to look at him he was staring at her. She flushed with heat and turned away. 'You shouldn't say things like that.'

'I'm simply admiring the view.'

'It's that way,' she said, pointing away from herself and turning away from him so that she could pull her phone out once more and take more photos of this stunning place. 'And you said you wouldn't do this.'

She knew what he was doing. He was trying to pull her back in. Maybe not all the way, but a little. Because it was familiar, that was all. And they both knew how much fun they could have between them. Out here, away from the medical bay in the glorious sunshine and the beautiful views, relaxing, chilling, it was too easy to forget all the stuff that made them impossible. And hadn't he kissed her recently and known it was a mistake? So flirting with her was wrong, too. It was downright cruel.

He had walked away. He had kissed her and called it a mistake. It was as if in kissing her like that—getting what he wanted in that moment and then apologising—he had got what *he* wanted and *he* needed, but her wants and desires had been completely ignored.

She had loved this man once. She had thought she had found her soul mate. But clearly he had never felt the same and she needed to remember that pain every single time she was tempted by him.

'You're right. I'm sorry,' he said.

It wasn't enough. Despite her thoughts earlier, she couldn't help but ask. 'Nate, why did you leave, without a word?'

'Maddy—'

'Did I not deserve an explanation?'

Nate sighed and looked down at the ground. 'I didn't think. I wasn't thinking clearly back then. There was a family emergency and I had to go. By the time my brain wasn't so muddled, so many months had passed and it just seemed easier to stay away. I mean, we were only casual, weren't we?'

She nodded, but internally she was screaming. She wanted to let him know that for her their relationship had been something far more serious than casual. That she had fallen in love with him. That the sex had been great, of course, but that that wasn't all that had drawn her to him. He was funny, kind and, she'd thought, loyal. He'd been intelligent and caring and he'd had her back at work. He'd been her best friend. 'Tell me what happened.'

He shrugged. 'It's complicated.'

'We have all day together. I'm happy to listen. Maybe if I understood then it wouldn't bother me as to why you walked away without telling me. Did you not think I deserved a second thought? Some consideration?'

He laid his hand on hers. 'Of course I did. But things moved so fast, and I barely had time to sort things out with the hospital. Every second mattered and I had to make choices. Prioritise.'

'And I wasn't one?' She pulled her hand out from under his.

'I'm not saying that.'

'Then what are you saying?'

Nate sighed. 'Like I said, it's complicated. You'd have to know my family to understand.'

'How could I have known about your family? You told me nothing. I didn't even know you had a brother until I met him the other day.'

'I told you that me and my family didn't speak. Lucas and I were estranged, so no, I chose not to tell the colleague I was having casual sex with about my very personal past!'

Maddy flushed and looked around them. Anyone could hear! Thankfully, it seemed no-one was listening, or if they were they were doing a very good job of hiding it. 'Fine. Don't tell me if I was just a colleague to you.' She walked away from him and over to the other side of the viewing point, trying to let go of her hurt and instead absorb the raw beauty of nature that she could see from up here, allow it to soothe her. They were in a magical place. She should be in awe. But instead she was hurting.

She busied herself taking photos. She got a couple to take a picture of her by the railing, then thanked them and returned the favour. When she checked her phone and compared the photo the couple had taken to the photo Nate had taken, she could see a huge difference.

She looked happy in Nate's photo, stilted in the second one.

Why do I let him have such power over me?

Maddy stalked over to him. 'Look, this is ridiculous! We're in this beautiful place. Let's not make it ugly by raking over the past. What's happened has happened and neither of us can change it, no matter how much we want to. The captain told us to rest and enjoy ourselves, so can we agree to just get on with that?'

Nate nodded. 'Of course. Shall we head back down—find a place on the beach or the sand dunes to have our picnic?'

Maddy agreed and forced a smile. 'That sounds wonderful. Let's do that.'

Nate had asked the kitchen to put together a few things for their little picnic and as he pulled out the sandwiches Maddy smiled.

'Egg and cress? You hate it!'

He winked at her. 'I've grown to love it.'

She remembered their first day in the emergency department together at London Saint Hospital. It had been their first shift and they'd been shadowing the same doctor, who'd been rushed off his feet. It was the middle of the afternoon before he'd even thought to tell them to go and have thirty minutes for their lunch break.

Their heads had been swimming with information. It was one thing to sit in a lecture room and learn about the human body, but quite another actually to be in the action of a real Accident and Emergency department and be responsible for people's lives. It had been overwhelming, but they'd both been buzzing as they'd made it up to the cafeteria in the hospital to grab a quick snack and the only sandwiches left in the fridge had been egg and cress.

'Ooh, lovely!' Maddy had said, grabbing them, along with a packet of crisps from the selection offered and a bottle of water.

'You like egg and cress?' he'd asked.

'I love it! You don't?'

He'd ended up having to grab cold chicken pasta in a plastic container, as it had been the only thing left, along with a badly bruised apple and a plain vanilla yoghurt. It hadn't exactly been dining like kings, but it'd had to do. He'd figured they were lucky to get a break at all, with the department having been so busy with patients. His chicken pasta had been tasteless, bland, and he'd pushed it to one side and eyed the yoghurt with apprehension.

'Here…have one of mine.' Maddy had offered him one of her sandwiches.

'No, no. That's yours. One of us should eat.'

She'd leaned forward then and made him make eye contact. 'No, we both should eat, or we're going to drop like flies. And those people sitting in that A&E waiting room are depending upon people like us to be at the top of our game. We can't be that if we don't eat properly.'

'Okay.' Reluctantly, he'd taken the sandwich and had had to admit that it wasn't half bad. She'd shared her crisps with him and they'd sat there discussing their morning, laughing about the moment when he'd struggled to get a cannula in because his hands had been shaking. And about the female patient who had come in with a fever and low belly pain and how Maddy had suspected a urinary tract infection. She'd asked her patient for a water sample and left her to it, returning moments later to find a sample filled with beautifully clear water. Maddy had thought the woman extremely well hydrated, until the female patient had held up the water bottle she'd been drinking from and said, 'I hope this brand is okay. It's not the one I normally drink.'

Realisation had dawned rather quickly!

'Oh God, do you remember those days? We were so enthusiastic! So young!' Maddy said as she helped him lay out the picnic now.

'So naïve.'

She laughed. 'We had no idea what was ahead of us, did we?'

'Nope.' Now he smiled. 'It was a steep learning curve, that's for sure. I remember going home each day and flopping onto the sofa, absolutely shattered.'

Maddy nodded. 'I remember one day, I had a day shift. Seven in the morning until five. Five minutes before the end of my shift and I'm called into Resus to assist with the incoming patients from a large road-traffic accident—five patients, all in various states of injury, all serious. I finally left the hospital a few minutes to midnight and I got into my car and thought I'd just close my eyes for a few minutes before I drove home. Next thing I knew, you were rapping your knuckles against the driver window and it was minutes before our next day shift.'

He laughed, remembering, shaking his head. 'You'd been there all night!'

'You gave me your banana and the rest of your mocha.' She smiled. 'If only you'd had a toothbrush and toothpaste on you.'

'Sadly, I didn't carry that as standard.' He laughed.

'You looked out for me from that day onwards.'

'You had my back too,' he said, smiling at her.

Those early days had been hectic. Foundation year doctors had to learn so many things that they just didn't get taught in a university lecture room. They'd had one lecture on how to deliver bad news to a patient and, whilst theory had been good in hypothetical situations, when it came to actually telling someone in real life that their family member had cancer or had died, people didn't always react the way they'd been told in books or lecture notes.

He'd always struggled with how long he ought to sit with someone after delivering bad news. He'd felt he should stay, answer questions and be there for them if needed. But in a busy A&E department he'd been needed elsewhere. Someone might just have lost a father, a mother, a wife, husband or child, but all the other patients had needed him too, so he'd not been able to stay with grieving family members or patients for as long as he would have liked.

There'd been one couple who'd come in with their daughter, a type-one diabetic who had gone into a diabetic coma at home. They had tried their best to revive her, but it had been too late and there'd been nothing they could do. The little girl had been ten years old, an only child. An IVF baby: precious, wanted and adored. Their reason for being had gone and they'd both collapsed in grief in the family room as he'd delivered the news. He'd taken them to her and stood with them, head bowed, as they had told her how much she was loved. And all the time his beeper had been going off, demanding his attention, calling him to other things deemed urgent.

There'd never been a lecture about *that*. The shame he'd felt, standing there as that beeper had interrupted those grieving parents over and over again… The embarrassment he'd felt to have had to make his excuses and leave them to it…

Maddy had covered for him as much as she could. She'd known where he was and had instructed the nurses to beep her for his patients and his patients' results, so that he'd be able to spend time with that couple, but even she hadn't been able to do everything. And, when he'd finally left them to return to his work and paste on a smile for others, he'd noticed the vast array of work that Maddy had got through—along with that for her own patients—just so that he could give his time to the grieving parents.

'Your colleagues become family. You can't help it,' she said.

'Sometimes they become something more,' Nate said, thinking of how his feelings towards fellow medic Maddy had changed. 'Sometimes they see them at a party in a beautiful red dress and realise the most gorgeous woman in the world has been by their side all the time.'

She blushed, even now. 'And they take you by the hand and lead you down a garden path…'

The party had been for a colleague having a thirtieth birthday party. His parents had offered to let him throw it at their place, which had turned out to be some large house in Surrey.

Somehow, miraculously, the party had fallen on a rare weekend on which neither Maddy nor Nate had been working and so they'd been able to go. Sick to death of scrubs and having her hair twisted up onto the top of her head, Maddy had taken the opportunity to go all out, to feel like a woman again. She'd worn a red dress that had emphasised her bust and hips and a hemline that had revealed her long legs. She'd worn her hair down and tamed into luscious waves, with smoky eye make-up and a black choker at her neck. She'd wanted to walk into the party and have all eyes turn to her, for the men that she worked with to realise that there was more to her than bags under her eyes, hair that hadn't been washed for a while and a strong pair of arms capable of popping a dislocated shoulder back into its socket.

She'd wanted to feel feminine, she'd wanted to feel attractive, and, yes, she'd wanted to capture

Nate's eye most of all. They'd been spending so much time together and she liked him—liked him a lot. But all they'd ever seemed to do when they'd had spare moments together was complain about how tired they were and how much they just needed a quick catnap, or the ability to go to the toilet whenever they wanted.

'It's so hypocritical!' she'd said. 'We sit there lecturing patients on staying hydrated and making sure they eat properly and I'm sat there having not eaten or drunk anything for over twelve hours straight!

Maddy had planned to drink whatever she wanted at the party, eat whatever she wanted and dance the night away. She'd wanted to have fun, to kick back, to relax—and why shouldn't she? she'd thought. She'd been putting in so much overtime at work that very often she'd barely made it home. That weekend, that party, had been for her to remember who she used to be.

The Surrey house had ben amazing. At the end of a large, sweeping driveway, the house had seemed more of a manor than anything else. There'd been butlers handing out drinks when she'd arrived—butlers!—and she'd taken a flute of champagne and entered. She'd realised that birthday boy Rupert really hadn't been lying about Mummy's and Daddy's pad in the country.

Music had blared and she'd followed the noise towards a room that had been packed, not only with medics, but people she hadn't known—Rupert's friends and family, presumably. A radiologist she knew had noticed her and waved, mouthing that Maddy looked gorgeous. She'd smiled and moved on, looking for Nate, and then she'd seen him, dressed in a dinner suit, laughing and joking with the birthday boy himself.

Rupert had noticed her first and then Nate had turned to see what had drawn his friend's eye. Maddy had felt thrilled inside when she'd seen Nate's eyes widen in shock and admiration as she drew closer.

'What vision do I see before me?' asked Rupert, laughing, clearly already drunk, dropping an air kiss either side of her face.

'Happy birthday, Rupe.' She passed him a small gift-wrapped box, tied with a bow.

'You look amazing,' Nate said, drawing in to drop a real kiss onto her cheek. She'd blushed.

'I'm going to take this over to the present pile!' Rupert said, holding the gift in the air and making his way through the throng of guests.

'There's a pile?' she asked with a raised eyebrow.

'Looks like it. He's a popular guy.'

'More popular now everyone knows he's rich.' She laughed.

'Lot of surprises tonight. Rupert is practically an earl and you…you are bloody stunning! Come dance with me!'

'Alright.' She smiled, hoping it was demurely, and allowed him to take her hand and lead her out onto the dance floor. She dropped her now empty champagne flute onto a passing tray and, facing Nate, began to move to the music. He was a great dancer, in tune with his body. He threw some shapes, making her laugh, and then all of a sudden the music changed and became slower and Nate smiled at her, took her hand and drew her into his embrace.

She laid her head against his shoulder and began to realise that something was changing between them. To be fair, she'd felt her feelings towards him change quite a lot just recently. They were still the friends and colleagues they had always been, but she'd begun to notice things lately: how his smile made her feel; how his laughter lifted her mood; how just being around him soothed her soul. He had a cute smile. He was easy on the eye, and she'd noticed how the nurses and other people looked at him. He was effortlessly good-looking, even with bedhead, which was how he often rolled into work.

And now, with her body up close to his, her awareness of him increased. Her heart thumped wildly in her chest and she kept trying to calm it down. Her pulse pounded in her ears as much as the music did. She was aware of the way he had his hand wrapped around hers, and how his other hand lay on the small of her back, very close to the top curve of her bottom.

She kept wondering what it might feel like to kiss him.

And then the moment was lost as the music changed again, someone bumped into them and dragged Nate away to see something and Maddy was left in the centre of the dance floor feeling bereft and alone.

She ended up chatting with other people, but she found herself constantly looking for him and, when she couldn't stand not seeing him again for another moment longer, she went looking for him, searching the crowd and the thronging dance floor. And, just when she thought that maybe he'd left without saying goodbye, a hand enclosed her own and turned her around…and there he was, smiling, eyes sparkling as he dragged her out of the room and down a corridor, through a doorway and out onto a patio lit by the stars in an inky sky above.

She could still hear the music, but out here in the gardens it was muted and cooler. Nate led her down some steps, across the grass and over to a stone folly that stood in the centre of the garden. 'Our own dancefloor. Less crowded,' he said, still holding her hand as he pulled her close once again.

Maddy smiled back at him. 'You want to show me some more moves?'

'I've got plenty.'

'Oh yeah?'

'Yeah. Want to see them?'

He was teasing her and she liked it. 'Of course.'

Nate laughed and stood back to admire her in her dress. 'I have never seen a woman look so beautiful as you do tonight.'

'Just tonight?' she teased. 'Wow, thanks. You're going to have to do better than that, you know.'

But then he stared into her eyes, mirth in his gaze that slowly turned serious as they stood in the dark folly. Shadows encompassed his face as they moved slowly to the muted music, occasionally the moonlight gifting her light to see the look of desire in his eyes.

Her mouth went dry as her gaze dropped to his lips. She had thought about kissing Nate; of course she had! Many times. She'd wondered what it might be like. He was a handsome man; clever; kind. He was her best friend at the hospital and she'd always been wary of overstepping that boundary.

But tonight it was as if there was magic in the air, anticipation. Electricity sparked as they gazed into each other's souls. She was aware of every touch: how his hand held hers as they danced; where their bodies met; the heat of him; the feel of him. And, for just a moment, they weren't friends, colleagues or doctors but two adults dancing in the dark, softly swaying in the moonlight, gazing into each other's eyes and thinking incredibly naughty things they could do to one another.

Nate made a little groan as he looked at her.

'What?' she asked. 'Tell me what you're thinking.'

'I'm thinking that I want to have you, but I'm wary of ruining our friendship and…now I'm aware that, just by saying it, I may have changed something between us. Have I?'

Of course he had. But by telling her that he wanted her too he had made her heart explode with joy. They both felt the same thing! 'If I said I wanted you too…what would that mean?' she whispered.

He smiled. 'Everything.'

She could feel his arousal pressed up against her as they softly moved, swaying from side to side.

'I don't want to make it awkward at work,' he said.

Maddy smiled. 'Neither do I.' She'd had enough people let her down. She didn't need to lose him. Apart from work, he was the most important thing in her life. He was her everything.

'Then if we do this there should probably be some rules,' he said, nuzzling at her neck, as if he couldn't bear not to touch her. As if he needed to sample her, taste her.

She could feel his breath upon her neck, and the brush of his lips was electrifying. Every nerve ending tingled delightfully.

'Okay,' she breathed, tilting her head to the side to reveal her neck more, to submit.

'Friends first but…with benefits.'

She felt his tongue lick her skin.

Maddy murmured assent, unable to think, not really processing what she had agreed to. Even afterwards she reckoned it would change, because what they had was so great, but in that moment she would have agreed to anything.

And then his hands were exploring her, his lips met hers and, before she knew what was happening, he moved aside her underwear and they were having sex up against the wall of the folly.

It was hot, fast and furious and she couldn't

get enough of him as he thrust inside her. She gasped, gripping him to her, looking up at the sky and the moon high above, hearing the hoot of an owl as she wrapped her legs around his body and tried to ignore the feel of the stone on her back, which was uncomfortable, but she didn't care in the moment.

Afterwards, panting heavily, they both laughed at each other, realising how crazy they'd been; anyone could have seen them! They adjusted their clothes and tried to look less rumpled as they returned to Rupert's party just in time for his speech, before he cut the massive cake that no doubt had been baked for him by some celebrity chef or something.

Maddy kept catching Nate's gaze and they smiled at one another.

And she believed it was the beginning of something exciting, something special.

And she hoped, naively as it turned out, that he felt the same way…

Cies Island was amazingly beautiful. The kind of place that took a person's breath away. That took all their cares and worries and made them forget them as they took in the views, breathed the clean air and gazed at the blue skies and along the white, sandy beaches, realising that all those concerns didn't really matter in that moment. They could return to them later, but right then they should enjoy, relax, sunbathe or paddle barefoot in the sea, jump the gentle waves. Let the warm rays of the sun caress the skin and just chill.

Maddy tried to do that. She tried to forget the fire in the kitchen, the fire in Nate's recent kiss and the fire in her soul that fuelled her confusion about him. Would she ever be clear in her thoughts about him? Would she ever douse the flames of her attraction to him? Could she get the furnace currently burning down to a spark, a small, tiny, glowing ember, and then stamp it out somehow?

She felt that, if she could, then this, right here, right now, would be so much easier. They'd just be two old friends who knew each other and had reunited for a work contract. She'd feel glad to see him and to be back with him, but that was all it would be, and she could explore the ports and make new friends and regain her confidence in her job and find her footing once again. She was getting there. She could feel it. There was less apprehension now, seeing her patients, and she could feel her old self coming back. But her old self had let him kiss her and call it a mistake. In the past, this man had slept with her on multiple occasions and then had left without a word. How could she feel safe with him? He'd not earned her trust.

'Do you regret what we had?' he asked, looking at her from across the small blanket he'd brought.

She shook her head. 'No, I don't. Being with you like that, even for a short time, made me very happy indeed. You made me feel wanted and I'd not felt that before, so…no, no regrets for that part. But I do regret allowing my feelings to become something more than our original rules stated for our relationship.' She blushed.

He sat forward and gazed at her. 'What?'

He'd not known? She'd thought he knew! Or at least suspected… 'You didn't know?'

'No! I mean, I knew we got on really well, and we were great friends and you really liked spending time with me, but I never dreamed for one moment that…' He trailed off, his gaze focused out to sea, as if regretting a life decision.

Did he regret it? 'So I felt very upset when you left without a word. In fact…' She swallowed her pride and decided to hit him with the truth. Maybe then he'd understand why she kept bringing the subject up, despite her request for them to forget it, because that was impossible. 'In fact, your leaving…it broke me a little. Hurt me *a lot*. It took me a long time to get over you going.'

Nate kept shaking his head as if in disbelief, then he turned to her. 'I'm sorry.'

'For leaving?'

He nodded. 'I'm sorry for leaving you and I'm sorry for not realising that I'd hurt you. I honestly believed that you'd just move on, that you'd be fine. You never said a word about… how you felt.'

Maddy smiled. 'How could I? Every time in my life that I'd hoped for more from someone, hoped for commitment, I was disappointed. I thought I might scare you off; you were so determined to stand alone and not have feelings for anyone. You just wanted the fun, without the scary part, so I gave you that.'

'I feel terrible. I'm sorry.'

'It was a long time ago,' she said, trying to cut him some slack, even though the pain of it still felt raw. But at least he'd apologised now. At least he'd finally admitted that what he'd done was wrong and that he'd never meant to hurt her. And honestly, if he truly hadn't known about her more romantic feelings for him, why would he have suspected that his leaving would hurt her? He'd have just assumed she'd say *adiós* and move on.

'Have you met anyone since?' he asked.

She shook her head. 'Our jobs don't leave us much time for romance. I've dated, but the relationships never really become anything. Not a lot of people are happy to know that they come second to our jobs, or that we'll miss special occasions really often, arrive late or not at all, and generally let them down all the time. How about you?'

'Same. I've dated, but it's hard to prove to someone that they're important, when patient care and the demands of a hospital take precedence every single time. Maybe that's why a lot of medics turn to other medics—because they know that that person will understand.'

Maddy nodded.

Nate laughed. 'I can't believe it. What a pair we've both turned out to be. We both leave London Saint and we both end up working on the same cruise ship. It's a small world.'

'And I want to see every corner of it,' she told him.

'You will. Listen, I accept that I made a lot of mistakes in the past, and I wouldn't blame you if you hated me for ever because of them, but...can we agree to live for the present and just enjoy what we have now?'

'And what do we have now?'

'I would like to think respect and admiration for one another. I would like to hope for friendship. But, if that's too much, then I'll understand.'

She couldn't hate him. That could never happen. 'Friends. I can do that,' she said.

Nate smiled and held out his hand for her to shake.

She shook it, trying to ignore how it felt to touch him once again. Maybe *friends* might still be a little bit of a stretch...

CHAPTER SIX

THINGS WERE GREAT for the next week. Maddy and Nate were on their best behaviour with one another: perfect colleagues, bright, happy; working well together. They'd moved on from Vigo to Lisbon, then Gibraltar and, most recently, Palma. Maddy had left the ship each time to explore the ports and always brought a little something back with her to remind herself of the place.

In Lisbon she'd bought a little *azulejo* tile to use as a coaster in her cabin. In Gibraltar, she'd bought a little keyring with a Barbary macaque on it. And in Palma a beautiful leather belt to go with a white *broderie anglaise* dress that she owned. She wanted to own a little piece of every place to which she went, to claim it and remember the happy memories she had of wandering their streets. She'd felt for a long time that she didn't actually have very many happy memories and it was time she made some. She was fed up with just reacting to life. She wanted to be proactive, make her own happiness and stop waiting for happiness to happen *to her*. So she explored, she made new friends, she worked hard and she went and checked on Manuel and the other chefs who were now back in the ship's cleaned and refitted crew mess.

So she was in a good mood when a passenger came limping into the medical bay, looking for help. He was an older gentleman with hair greying at his temples and, because he was wearing shorts, she could easily see what his problem was straight away. He had quite the swollen knee, and she helped him to a bed in one of the bays.

His name was Michael Stanton. 'It felt a little achy yesterday, but I woke up this morning with it looking like this.'

'Have you had an injury recently—slipped, fallen, banged it?'

He shook his head. 'No. Nothing like that.'

'And the swelling appeared overnight?'

'Yes.'

'And the pain, how would you describe that? Is it an ache? Is it burning, or sharp?'

'It was very sudden…severe. It woke me up.'

'And have you had any problems with this knee before, with issues like this or otherwise?'

'I damaged it once playing cricket—a ball

smacked into it—but that was when I was a teenager. It's always been a little achy since then.'

'And would you say the pain is localised to this joint only? What about your hips or ankles?'

'Maybe in my big toe. That hurts like a…' He flushed a little. 'Like hell. Swelled up too once before.'

Maddy examined both of his legs, comparing them. The left knee had less movement and caused Mr Stanton considerable pain. Plus it looked quite red and felt warm. 'Any fever or chills?'

'A bit tired, and I always run warm anyway.'

She took his temperature. It was slightly raised, indicating a low fever.

'What's your diet like generally?'

He chortled. 'I eat well!' He slapped his belly, which hung slightly over his belt. 'Must admit I have a taste for fine things.'

She smiled. 'And I bet you've been indulging on board!'

'It's what holidays are for, enjoying yourself! Last night I had the finest surf and turf I have ever eaten in my life: medium-rare T-bone steak, langoustines, washed down with the wonderful rioja.'

'Sounds amazing. Now what about medications? Do you take anything?'

'Just aspirin every day. My doctor recommended it.'

'And any medical conditions I should know about?'

'Type-two diabetes. I'm working on it, trying to eat right, but… I'm on holiday! I'm allowed a little time off the diet, right?' He gave her a nudge with his elbow.

She smiled and said nothing. A lot of patients thought that they could abandon their diets on holiday and found that it led to a bit of a deterioration in their wellbeing. Examining him, she confirmed the swelling and redness was confined to the knee. The skin looked shiny, as if stretched, and it felt hot to the touch. There was bulging either side of the patella and Mr Stanton had reduced movement and pain. And, when she removed his shoes, she found he did indeed have the same affliction on his left big toe and she could feel crystals beneath the skin: tophi.

'Well, it looks, Mr Stanton, like you have gout in the knee joint and your large toe on this side. I'd like to confirm it with a needle aspiration to obtain some of the synovial fluid. This will confirm diagnosis and rule out any infection, and may even reduce some of your pain by relieving the pressure in the joint.'

‘*Gout?* But my dad had that. Isn’t it an old man’s disease?’

‘No, it can affect anyone, but now I know that you have a family history that makes the diagnosis even more likely. But I’d like to aspirate just to make sure we don’t have any septic arthritis happening.’

‘Oh. Okay. Will it hurt?’

‘No, I can do it under a local anaesthetic.’

‘Oh…right…well, I guess you better do that, then.’

‘It’ll just take me a moment to gather everything. Stay here and I’ll be straight back.’ She smiled and left him in his cubicle to gather the antiseptic solution, sterile equipment, anaesthetic, needle, syringe and the containers she’d need to place the sample in. She arranged it all onto a trolley and then pushed it back into Mr Stanton’s bay. He seemed to be staring past her shoulder, looking slightly aggrieved, a change from his previous happy-go-lucky attitude.

Maddy glanced to look behind her and saw Nate talking to one of their nurses. ‘Everything okay, Mr Stanton?’

‘You know him?’ He indicated with his head towards Nate.

‘Dr Blake? Yes, of course.’

‘Nathaniel. Hmm. You need to keep an eye

on him. I wouldn't trust him as far as I could throw him.'

Maddy turned to look at Nate, then back at her patient. 'Why?' Afterwards, she would berate herself for having asked, but in the moment, she was surprised and curious.

'Took me a moment to recognise his face, but… I knew his family back in the day. Always causing trouble for his parents, and when his brother needed him by his side he never came home. Abandoned him. He just didn't care! Thought he was above them…and him a doctor, too. You'd expect him to care more about the ones he's meant to love.' Mr Stanton leaned in. 'If you want my advice, I'd keep your distance, because that man only cares about himself.'

Maddy frowned. Was that true? Had Nate abandoned his brother in a time of need? Abandoned his parents? She knew he'd abandoned her once, so maybe this was what Nate was like. Maybe she ought to be more careful and less naïve in believing his promises…but she'd seen for herself that Nate and Lucas were great. So was what Mr Stanton said lies? Or had Nate and Lucas made amends? Maybe the reason Nate had left her all those years ago was to sort out his relationship with his brother. Because they were here together on this ship and they were close…or at least, seemed to be.

The idea that there was still so much she didn't know about Nate niggled at her. He had always been a closed book and kept her at an arm's length when it came to anything about his past or his family. Maybe this was why. Was he ashamed at how he'd treated them, and thought that she might judge him if she knew? He'd still only given her the bare minimum of an explanation about what had happened.

Should I go and talk to Lucas? No. That would be going behind Nate's back. I have to talk to Nate.

But, as she performed the needle aspiration on Mr Stanton's knee, her own doubts began to surface, her mind muddied by her patient's comments about Nate's past. Was she repeating patterns of getting involved with someone unavailable to her? All her life, even as a kid growing up in care, she'd pinned her hopes on other people making her happy. She'd hoped that she would get fostered. She'd hoped that she would one day get adopted. She'd hoped that she would one day be loved and cherished and put first.

But it had never happened. She'd always been let down by others, and here she was, hoping that this time with Nate they might be happy if only she put to one side her doubts, her fears and the fact that he had already shown her how he was going to treat her. He'd abandoned her once. He'd kissed her here on the ship and made her think for one brief moment that there was still something there between them, then had backed away, telling her it was a mistake. The man blew hot and cold. How much longer would she let him do that to her?

I need to grow a spine. Nate looks after himself and I need to do the same!

Cagliari was a beautiful port with gorgeous blue skies and calm, clear waters. Nate asked Maddy if he could accompany her when she disembarked.

'I was going to look at the citadel on the top of the hill—the Castello district,' she said.

'Sounds great.' He was keen to make sure that the two of them were okay. She'd seemed a little distant yesterday afternoon and evening and, if he had done something, he wanted to show her how important she still was to him, even though the two of them were just friends.

The citadel was made of pale stone that helped reflect the soaring heat of the day and had ramparts, battlements, domes and towers. The ground was cobbled and uneven, so he offered Maddy his arm as they walked, but she said she was fine.

She looked beautiful today. She looked beautiful every day, but today she looked even more so, in a long, flowing white dress, brown leather belt and sandals. Her hair was loose and flowing down her back, sometimes held off her face by the sunglasses she wore. The more time he spent with her, the more he regretted having walked away from her all those years ago, especially now he knew how she had felt about him, but he knew that if the same thing happened again, he would do the same thing. A fact that reminded him that he and Maddy were never meant to have been together and that somehow fate or the world was showing him this lesson even now.

They joined an organized tour of Il Castello, the citadel, exploring the cathedral and the ramparts, and gazing out at the views from the top of one of the towers of all Cagliari and the green trees of Sardinia. He could sense the history in a place such as this. It was dripping with it. He could imagine guards walking the corridors, prisoners down in the cramped, dark cells without the chance of freedom; armies trying to attack the walls.

Once the tour was done, they made their way to a small café and sat outside under a large purple umbrella, the tables covered in white PVC decorated with bright-red chilli peppers.

They ordered two aromatic coffees and a mandarin croissant each. Maddy had bought herself a trinket in a nearby gift shop—a beautiful filigree pendant with tiny blue stones.

'It's so beautiful here,' she said, leaning back in her chair and sighing. 'I wonder why I didn't take a cruise ship contract years ago. Would have saved me a lot of trouble and angst.'

'Well, first off, you need the experience in hospitals first, before you can be a cruise doctor.'

'Yeah, well, no-one tells you just how sometimes your dream of helping people can turn into a nightmare. But, if they told you from the get-go that you can help people and see the world and relax on a cruise ship?' She laughed. 'Maybe there'd be a lot more happier doctors.'

'You weren't a happy doctor?' he asked.

'I was, generally. But then you meet certain people and they pivot your life and change how you feel about something. How you feel about your job.'

Was she talking about him? Because back in the day they'd both seemed to love their job. He had so many memories of he and Maddy sharing smiles and laughter at work. Had she really lost her joy for the job after he'd left?

'Who did you meet?' he asked, curious to see if the reason she'd been cool since yesterday afternoon was because she'd been thinking about all the times he'd seemingly messed her around. 'Not me, I hope.' He laughed and sipped his coffee. It was dark, strong and bitter.

'There was a time when I wondered how I'd carry on without you. Especially as you'd been there with me since day one. But, no, I wasn't talking about you, but about someone else I met. Years after you—a patient, actually.'

'Oh?' He was curious. Some patients could really stay with a doctor. There could be a tragic story: cancers, brain tumours, children coming in with terminal diseases that they could do nothing for. It made him question being a doctor. Made him question if he was actually helping by prolonging their life with drugs, when he could see, as a doctor, that they were tired of it all. Of fighting every day in pain.

Maddy sucked in a breath and looked out over Cagliari. 'A guy in his twenties came in with abdominal pains. He was nauseous. Shaky. Dehydrated. We struggled to get fluids into him because his veins had collapsed and that was when we learned he was a drug addict in withdrawal. He was after pain meds and...' she paused to take a breath '...because I didn't give him what he wanted, as quickly as he wanted them, he became aggressive and cornered me. He pinned me to a wall, his arm against my throat, and then proceeded to physically attack me.'

'Maddy!' He couldn't believe it….well, unfortunately, he could. She'd been working in a central London emergency department; of course they were going to get drug-addicted patients in. It was par for the course, unfortunately, as was the risk of assault on staff. 'Were you okay?'

She shook her head. 'He fractured my orbital bone. My nose. Knocked out a tooth.' She tapped one of her front teeth and gave a wry smile. 'Security arrived a little too late and I was unconscious on the floor. I had to have surgery, and in recovery I started to have panic attacks. After that, I struggled with the idea of returning to work. I'd been in therapy for six months when I got the job on board *Serendipity.* My therapist had told me to find a way back and this is it—my way back to being a doctor. I love what I do, Nate, but I needed to feel safe, and I needed to have a life, and so this is what I chose. And in order to feel safe I have to have confidence in the people that I work with…and that includes you.

'But… I still don't know what happened with you. And yesterday I met a patient who knew your family. He told me some things and it's made me wonder if I can trust you. I want to. But I've already been hurt and damaged so much, and I don't want that to happen here, because this is my way back to reclaiming my power over my own life. And you? You're a threat. Do you understand?'

He nodded, shocked, appalled by what she had been through! If he had known…

What would I have done—abandoned Lucas and gone running back?

No. He would have felt torn. Lucas had needed him and he'd promised him that he would stay by his side until he was stronger. If he'd run out on him because Maddy had needed him he'd have hated himself, because he'd made his brother a promise never to do so again. 'I never knew you got hurt,' he said. 'I'm so sorry.' And who the hell was the patient who had known his family? And what had they said to her?

'Can you tell me the truth, Nate? You've never given me a full answer and I think…no, I *deserve*…the truth from you.'

He wanted to give it, but how could he tell her everything? He'd made a promise to his brother. But maybe he could give her fragments of the truth and leave certain parts out to protect Lucas. To protect *Maddy.*

'When I was really young, it was just me and my mum. My real dad passed when I was a baby. My mum was great, but she was lonely, and then she met this other guy who became my stepdad—Bill. Mum adored him. Was completely in love, even though Bill tried to hide the fact that he wasn't best pleased to be raising another guy's kid.'

'What happened?'

'Mum got pregnant and had Lucas.'

'He's your *half*-brother, then?'

He nodded. 'I loved having a baby brother, but Bill made it clear that I was second best in his eyes. I could do no right. I was often punished by him, and my mum began to take his side in the arguments. We used to be *so close* and suddenly with Bill and Lucas around I lost her. Me and Lucas, though, we were great, until he started to get older. With Bill's favouritism and Mum's enabling of Bill's behaviour, me and Lucas got pitted against one another. There were arguments, rows. I would stay out as often as I could, because home was a terrible place to be. Mum and Bill were drinkers by this time, and that made everything worse, so I left home when I could. Went to university and never looked back. Lucas stopped talking to me and I just assumed he'd had his head turned by Mum and Bill.'

'I'm so sorry. I never had any idea. Why didn't you tell me before?'

'It was a part of my past I didn't want to remember. I felt like I'd lost everyone I'd ever cared for. Even my home. You, my job, working at London Saint—that was all that mattered.'

'But then something pulled you back. What?'

Nate sighed. He hated that he had to bring up such ugliness in a place that was so beautiful. 'Lucas was struggling privately. I didn't know at the time, because we weren't speaking, but I found out that he'd been struggling with his sexuality, and when he came out to Mum and Bill they didn't accept him and threw him out. They were out in their car one day, and they'd been drinking, and got into an accident that killed them both.'

This was the part from which he'd have to divert some of the truth and use omission. 'Lucas couldn't deal with it and he called me and I left London Saint to help him.'

Maddy gazed at him with such sorrow and softness. 'I'm so sorry that you lost your mum and Bill that way. So that's why you left!'

He nodded. 'I needed that time to reconnect with my brother. We were all we had left.'

She reached forward then and laid her hand on his, squeezing his fingers. 'I'm so sorry.'

He liked the feel of her hand upon his, her reassuring touch, but he felt bad because he was still keeping some of the truth from her. ‘Thank you. It took some time but…here we are! Lucas and I are close again; we’ve got each other’s backs. And whoever that patient was who told you they recognised me and that you weren’t to trust me or whatever, they didn’t know the full story, and they most certainly did not understand what went on behind the closed doors of my childhood home.’

‘No-one ever can. We’re all fighting battles that no-one can see, aren’t we?’

‘I’m sorry I never contacted you. I was just overwhelmed with everything I had to process. The loss of Mum. Lucas.’ That was the truth. He had been overwhelmed by coping with the loss of his mother, learning that Bill had caused the accident from drink driving and essentially killed her. And discovering his little brother had actually not been able to handle any of it, had taken a drug overdose and was an addict with a history of hospital and rehab admissions.

It had been so much to take in, so much to deal with! And Lucas had fought so hard so get clean this time and return to a passion he’d had as a child—ice-skating. It was something he’d done in secret, because Bill had hated that his son was into that and not something Bill considered more manly. Ice-skating had begun to replace the drugs Lucas was addicted to, and with his brother's support he'd got a job on a cruise ship as an ice-dancer and Nate had gone along for the ride—not just to be with his brother, but to keep an eye on him. To be close, to give him support and rebuild what they'd once had all those years ago.

Too much had been taken from them and Nate had wanted to reclaim their lives. And he had—they had. And now Lucas was engaged to Carlos and it was time for Nate to let someone else take the reins in his brother's life. He would always be there for Lucas, but he had to let the guy stand alone too and have space. He was so happy that his brother had found someone to love after all that he had been through, and Carlos was amazing, perfect for his little brother. And now it was time for Nate to start thinking again about his own happiness, having put his own life on pause for so long.

So sue me if I kissed this beautiful woman after I'd had one too many to drink! He never drank, not really; just socially, and only one or two, but Lucas and Carlos had got engaged and that had been worthy of a celebration, as well as the fact that fate had brought Maddy back into his life and he'd like to think it was for a reason.

'Thank you for telling me, but now I know and the past is in the past, so shall we just move on? Take a moment to appreciate where we are? All of this?' She swept her arm wide, indicating the town of Cagliari far below, the beautiful dark green of the trees in the distance against an azure sky, the brilliant white of the cruise ship docked in the port against the clear blue waters; the happy people all around them; the good food on the table.

The company they kept.

Nate lifted his coffee cup in the air. 'To now and all its infinite possibilities.'

Maddy met his cup with her own, clinking it softly. 'The now.'

Her smile, when it came, warmed his heart immensely.

Nate's revelations in Cagliari were shocking, and she hated all that he had been through, but there'd been something in his delivery that had told her that he was still keeping something back, in the way he kept looking at her to see if she believed him. But what? And why didn't he feel he could trust her with it? It was why she had suggested they move on. That they stop dwelling in a past filled with secrets he wouldn't share and just accept where they were: in a beautiful place, in the here and now. Maddy was inwardly annoyed that she was being told half-truths, not trusted, and if he couldn't fully trust her how could she trust him?

You and I will always be together. Nate had said that to her once, when they'd been together at London Saint for about a year. *Fighting one accident and emergency at a time!*

She thought about that a lot as she returned to the medical bay the next day. They'd set sail from Cagliari about five the previous evening and woken up docked at Civitavecchia. Lots of passengers had disembarked and she was making her way through a crew clinic. She'd seen three patients so far, one for recurring migraine, one for a dislocated finger and her last patient for a follow-up after a previous accident, and she'd given them permission to go from light duties to full. She would call their supervisor later to confirm, but right now she had another ice-dancer in her clinic.

'The receptionist said I had to see *you* and not my brother.' Lucas looked over her shoulder towards his brother, who was leaning against a wall observing the consultation.

'The receptionist was right. What happened?' Nate asked.

Maddy turned to give him a stare. This was *her* consultation. 'Tell *me* what happened, please.'

'Good for you, Madeline. Put him in his place!'

Lucas smirked. 'It was stupid, really. I was doing a warm-up on the ice, slipped when I came off my edge and fell against a barrier. I've hurt my shoulder and I need you to tell me I have my shows, and a wedding!' He smiled at her and she saw Nate's features in his face. They had the same smile, cute and attractive, the kind that could charm birds from trees.

'Okay, let me take a look.' She examined him thoroughly, knowing that Nate was watching and would want a thorough assessment of his brother to make sure nothing was missed. Clearly he was protective. Lucas was developing swelling on his shoulder and had difficulty moving his arm and seemed to be in a lot of pain, despite his desire to drop quips and jokes into every bit of conversation they had. 'I think we need an x-ray,' she concluded. 'I can't feel a break, and there's no dislocation, but the x-ray will tell us for sure.'

'Will I be radioactive and get special powers?' he asked with a grin.

'Unfortunately not, but it will give *me* special powers to see inside your body, and I may even refer you to a clinic in Civitavecchia to get a CAT scan of the soft tissues.'

'Double radioactivity? Hmm. All I need is to get bitten by a spider and I'll turn into a superhero.'

Maddy laughed. 'No such luck, I'm afraid.'

'Damn, there's always a catch.'

Maddy performed the x-ray and Nate scanned it intensely. 'No break. He's been lucky.'

'Maybe a tear in his pectoralis major muscle?' she suggested.

'Possibly. What are you going to do?'

She frowned, amused by the way he was hovering, being overly concerned. She'd heard of helicopter parenting, but not with siblings. But maybe this was what family was like. They only had each other. 'Offer a sling and painkillers.'

'No. No painkillers.'

'Why?'

Nate shrugged. 'He won't take them. I know him.'

'Okay. He can tough it out then, but I'm still going to advise them.'

Back in the cubicle, she gave Lucas the results. 'I'm going to get you a sling for your arm to support it. I want you to rest it for a few days.'

'A sling? What colours do they come in?'

She smiled. 'Well, there's black, or you could choose…black.'

'Nothing with a bit of bling?'

'No, but I guess you could add that yourself if you wanted.'

'Honestly, Nate. You need to look at different stockists.'

'Not my choice,' Nate said with a smile.

Maddy began to put the sling on Nate's brother. 'So...you and Nate have a good evening the other night?'

'Oh, the best!' Lucas said. 'You missed a great night. You should have come! Why *didn't* you bring this wonderful woman, brother dear?'

'Lucas.'

'What?' Lucas asked innocently. 'Do you know, Maddy, that I asked him to be my maid of honour at the wedding and wear a nice dress, but he said the best he could do was wear a suit and be my best man. Honestly, what does a girl have to do to get a pretty bridesmaid?'

Maddy laughed as she tightened the straps, making sure the sling supported the arm perfectly. 'Maybe look elsewhere. Have you seen his legs? Not sure they're right for heels,' she joked.

Lucas looked at her weirdly then, his head tilted to one side. 'What about you?'

'I'm sorry?'

'You could be a bridesmaid! I know I've only met you twice, but Nate speaks very highly of you, and with that red hair of yours you'd look wonderful in pale green silk!'

'Oh, I don't know about—'

'Come on! Please?' he wheedled, then leaned in conspiratorially. 'You know I've heard that best men often get off with bridesmaids…'

Maddy flushed, aware that Nate was right there behind her and stepped away, laughing. 'I have no desire to get off with your brother!'

She could feel Nate's gaze upon her. She could feel his eyes boring into the back of her head. She was almost afraid to turn round. Had she hurt his feelings?

'Even so…what do you say?'

'I hardly know you. Don't you want to ask someone else?'

Lucas shook his head. 'I've got all my friends coming already. I want Nate to have someone there that he likes. Come on! Do it as a favour to me. Please?'

Her cheeks felt hotter than the sun, her mind whizzing with excuses and reasons not to do it. But what if she did? She'd never been part of a wedding before, never a bridesmaid. It might be fun to get dressed up and she liked Lucas a lot.

She nodded. 'Okay. I will.'

'He's asked the ship's captain to marry them, did you know?' Nate said, sliding into a booth opposite her in the crew mess.

'Really? That's nice. Is Captain Thomas going to do it?'

'Apparently he's happy to be part of it, though it will be more of a performance and symbolic. Lucas and Carlos want the excitement of being married on board and then getting the legal and official part done in Spain.'

'Am I going to have to be a bridesmaid at both?'

'I don't think so, but you'd better ask him.'

'If he really wants me, then I don't see why not. I came on board for new experiences and this would most certainly be one.'

Nate smiled. 'Then I'll see you at the other end of the aisle!' He got up and walked away and, whilst she was grateful that he'd not mentioned Lucas's 'getting off with the best man' comment, she couldn't help but imagine what it might be like to walk up an aisle with Nate at the other end…

Hadn't she once dreamed of it? Imagined it so perfectly in her head that she knew every detail? She knew what her dress would be like. How he would turn to look at her and openly cry as she walked towards him. She knew the flowers she'd hold. The way everyone would gaze at them—the perfect couple—and weep at the sight of such love.

She'd not allowed herself to remember that for such a long time: foolish, silly dreams of someone who often let her mind fly away on flights of fancy. She'd lived in her imagination as a child. What was so wrong in that? It was how she'd survived the disappointments of real life, imagining herself so loved, so cherished, about to embark on a journey of creating her own perfect family. That was why it had hurt so much when he'd walked away without a word of explanation or apology, as if she didn't matter. As if she wasn't important.

Only now she knew why he'd left, and realised how it had been nothing to do with her, but with a tragedy in his family and now she was being pulled into *their* family, *his* family. Nate's—as if her life was maybe destined to be forever entwined with his. Just not in the way she'd expected.

But, if Lucas wanted her as a bridesmaid, she'd do it to feel as though she belonged. To share in his day. To see that true happiness did happen to other people and that maybe, if she stayed in its orbit, then some of that happiness, well…might just rub a little of its magic onto her too.

As they sailed away from Civitavecchia, they received the report from the clinic on land: Lucas's CAT scan showed soft tissue damage, as suspected. He was told to rest for two days and then come back in for a check-up, to see if he could go on light duties.

He was not happy to miss out on shows, and Carlos had declared that Lucas was being insufferable because he was bored and couldn't work out. So Nate checked in with his brother each day and, when the swelling had gone down and the shoulder was feeling much better, Lucas returned to the ice show.

'You and Maddy ought to come and watch it!' Lucas enthused. 'You'll love it! It's a story of two lovers who can't be together and if the end dance—in which yours truly performs—does not leave you with tears in your eyes, then I won't have done my job!'

And so Nate asked Maddy to the ice show. When he went to meet her at her cabin, he tried not to be overwhelmed by how beautiful she looked. By her wonderful scent, the way her eyes sparkled as she took in his suit and open-necked shirt. How great it felt to walk down the corridor with her on his arm.

In the ice studio, they discovered that Lucas had reserved the two best seats in the house for them and they sat ringside, waiting for the lights to go down.

'This is exciting,' she said. 'Have you seen him skate before?'

'Many times. I took him to many training

sessions and sat ringside. I remember being cold a lot.'

'But impressed too, I bet?'

He nodded. 'He comes alive on the ice. You can see it in his eyes. He's so *present.* He looks the same way when he's with Carlos. That's how I know they're perfect for one another.'

She smiled at him, and when he met her gaze he wondered…*is that the same look I see in her eyes right now? Is she thinking I might be perfect for her?*

It sent a ripple of yearning through him of want, of possibility. His mind had been all over the place since he'd kissed her again and being by her side in the medical bay, working with her, spending time with her in ports and seeing her laugh and smile made him want to hold her all over again. The way the wind played with her loose hair, the way she made him feel about himself, made him want to feel her in his arms once more. There was something about the way the sun gleamed on her skin, that made him want to reach out and touch her, just to make sure that she was still as soft as he remembered.

And he remembered so much about her. The way she challenged him. The way they might meet each other's gaze in a serious staff meeting and try not to laugh. The way she sought him out to tell him something ridiculous, and the joy and fun in her eyes would sparkle with such a life of its own, it enthused her words with delight.

He remembered the way she felt beneath him; her soft gasps and moans of pleasure. The way she seemed to need him. How he could do so much with just the stroke of one finger…

He missed her. Even when he was with her, he missed her, because he couldn't have her the way that he wanted. Being with her in consultations was torture. His feelings for her had never truly gone away, but he didn't feel deserving of her. He'd failed his family. He'd failed his brother and he'd already failed her once too. He'd put her through so much; he'd hurt her and he didn't want to do that again. She didn't deserve that, so he was trying to keep his distance. Trying to honour the promise just to be friends, colleagues, nothing more.

But sitting with her like this, by her side in the dark, close enough to smell her delightful perfume, her leaning in to say something about the set on the ice, meant all he wanted to do was stare into her eyes, place his hand on the back of her neck and draw her face into his for a kiss.

The lights came up then went down again three times, signalling the start of the show, and music began to fill the room, haunting violin music, as a lone female skater emerged onto the ice.

He couldn't help but keep glancing at Maddy, watching Maddy's face as the ice show continued. He watched her delight, her rapt attention; the way she sometimes caught her bottom lip. He watched her smile, her joy, how she gasped when Lucas emerged onto the ice dressed as a monster, all fierce and cruel. She glanced back at him as if to say *it's your brother* and he smiled back and gripped the arms of the chair to stop himself from taking her hand in his. From grabbing her hand and leading her away from the ice studio, out into the bright corridors, down into the depths of the ship and to his cabin, then doing all the things his body was screaming at him to do.

But he didn't. He simply smiled back and maintained an image of calm on the outside, whilst internally he screamed. It was torture to sit next to the woman he yearned for and not be able to do anything.

Above everything, he respected her, admired her. She'd been attacked by a drug addict. His own brother had been one, and he'd made a promise to Lucas never to tell anyone about it. He'd made a promise to his brother that he would forever put him first, and he'd made a promise to *himself* that he would never hurt anyone the way he had hurt people before, and that meant not getting close to Madeline.

She would be hurt if she got involved with him again because he wasn't sure that he was good enough for her. Sure, there was a physical connection—they'd proved that before—but was there anything beyond it? Would she cheer his brother and clap for him the way she did now if she learned that Lucas had also once been addicted and had stolen to get money for drugs?

He'd accepted his brother had been a different person then. Life had forced him into a corner and the addiction had made him into someone he wasn't. *That* Lucas didn't exist any more, but would *she* accept that? Would she still be Lucas's bridesmaid if she knew that?

He tried to imagine Maddy in a bridesmaid dress. He saw her walking down an aisle in a beautiful dress and somehow his mind morphed her from being a bridesmaid into a bride, wearing a white dress and long veil, walking towards him.

His heart skipped a beat. He grew hot and he had to take a sip of his ice-cold drink to cool himself down.

As the finale of the show began and the music increased in power and volume, his gaze returned to the ice to honour his brother in the finale. Lucas skated with heart and passion and he could see how he emoted his feelings so clearly, now that he was no longer a monster but human, and how it felt to grieve a lost love that he could now no longer have.

Nate felt tears come to his eyes as, Lucas died from a broken heart on the ice. The lights changed, the music became ethereal and his lost love came to claim his soul so that they skated into the ever after together.

The idea that he could not be with the one he loved until after death… How heartbreaking.

The ice studio erupted in applause as everyone got to their feet, entertained and moved by the show, and the skaters all came onto the ice to accept the applause. Lucas even skated forward to have a hug with them both, and Nate noticed Maddy wipe her eyes.

'That was so moving!' Maddy said, crying and dabbing at her eyes with a tissue as they walked out. 'I've never felt that way before. Lucas was amazing! They all were amazing!' She half-laughed, slightly embarrassed at being so emotional.

'I guess he warned us.'

'Yes. Oh my goodness, should we go and get some fresh air? I think I need it.'

He led her up to the open deck. It was a beautifully warm night. The skies were clear and lit with stars as they cruised through the sea towards Malta.

'Lucas is so talented. You can see he adores what he does.'

'He really does,' Nate agreed.

'I want to feel that way about my work.'

'Don't you?'

She smiled. 'I enjoy what I do, but am I passionate about it? I think I'm still getting used to being back in work, though it has been nice for things to be less hectic than an A&E. I just wonder if there's more.'

'More what?'

'Ways to help people. Sometimes I feel like... Well, like I'd like to know how their story ends. It's great being on board, but it's so transient, isn't it? Passengers come and then they disappear.'

'I suppose.'

'Have you ever thought about putting down roots? Because I think about that all the time. As a child, I wanted a family more than anything, but I was never in the same place for more than a few months. Being at London Saint was the longest I'd stayed anywhere! And that would probably be where I would still be, if I hadn't been attacked.'

He nodded, listening carefully.

'Sometimes I have this dream about putting down proper roots. Setting up a clinic for women, maybe. But settling down and staying somewhere and making a difference to their lives and seeing that difference in the community.'

'And what about for you?'

She frowned. 'How do you mean?'

'Do you see yourself settled down with someone? Like, in a relationship?'

She smiled. 'It would be nice, if I was ever able to trust someone enough for that.'

'Would you ever trust me?'

She blinked and looked away out to sea. 'We said we'd just be friends, Nate.'

He nodded, disappointed, but supposed she was making the right decision. He had proved to this woman that he would only fail her and let her down. It was no wonder she couldn't contemplate anything like that with him. He needed to atone for his mistakes, and that meant not to keep pressing her into an uncomfortable corner.

But the vision she'd presented of settling down, a clinic in a small community so that it got that continuity of care, called to him. He'd felt so adrift for so long now, helping Lucas chase his dreams, supporting him, getting him back on his feet… It felt good to see his brother improve and make his life, but wasn't it now time for Nate to do the same? 'You should do that, if it's what you want. Settle somewhere. Start a family. I know that's always been your dream.'

She talked about it once, all those years ago, before they'd got intimate. About how growing up without a family, without any blood relatives, had made her crave her own, and how she dreamed that one day she'd find true love, settle down and have lots of little kids. And the best thing was he could envision her as a mother. She'd be amazing at it—she had such a big heart.

She nodded. 'It has. When I lay in that hospital bed after surgery, it made me realise how short life is. There was a moment during the attack when I thought I might die, that he might kill me. And how I was too young, and that my life hadn't really begun. How I'd experienced nothing! And I promised myself that if I made it through I would make changes. I would see the world. I would travel and I would seek out joy.'

'And so you came to the *Serendipity*.'

'Yes. And, though I love my job, for a long time now I've felt like there's something missing. I'm there for other people, but there's no-one there for me. An empty flat. An empty cabin. It makes you wonder just what you're doing and who you're doing it for.'

'You're not fulfilled?'

'Sometimes I feel so alone here, in the middle of the sea.'

'I'm here for you.'

She smiled. 'But you're just a friend, Nate. My boss. My colleague. I can't afford you to be anything else, because you broke my heart, and I'm not sure I can stand the risk of giving it to you again.'

She gave me her heart? 'We were just meant to be friends with benefits. No strings, we both said.'

Maddy gazed at him softly as a gentle breeze played with her hair. 'And I meant to keep it that way, only things changed for me. I fell for you, you fool! And then you just upped and left.'

He stared hard at her. He'd not known! If he had…

No, I can't think about that, because I know I would have gone to Lucas, but...

But he might have found a way to have both. Somehow, he might have found a way! The pain tore through him at the thought that he'd left her hurting, knowing now that her feelings for him had run a lot deeper than he'd ever imagined. The fact was that he'd begun to feel the same way about her, he'd been developing feelings, but his had terrified him!

I was a coward and Lucas's troubles gave me a way out.

Nate turned to her, reached for her hands and held them in his. 'I am *so sorry* that I left the way that I did. If I could go back and change it…'

'It's fine. Your brother needed you; I understand.'

'No! It's not fine! I…' He searched for the right words to say to her. To let her know just how much she had meant to him. How her friendship had meant everything. How being in her arms had soothed his soul. How much he used to look forward to being with her and having her all to himself. How he'd thought he couldn't tell her about his growing feelings because he'd definitely not been good enough for her back then.

He'd only given her the best of himself: fun Nate. The man behind the mask he'd worn to make himself feel good. The mask that had presented him to the world as a cool, confident doctor, fun and amiable, clever and dedicated, passionate and popular. When inside he'd felt as if he was crumbling. As if he was barely getting through each day, sometimes making mistakes. Fighting to prove to himself that he was more than Bill had told him he was—a nobody, not worthy of anyone's time or attention. Useless, a waste of space who no-one could ever love.

He'd grown up hearing nothing but negativity, and sometimes it was all he could believe. And his mother had died without him having got the chance to put things right between them; Lucas had almost overdosed… He'd vowed to atone for the abandonment of his brother and he thought he'd been doing a good job until he'd run into Madeline again and realised just how much he'd hurt her too.

'I wish I'd never hurt you, because you were so much more than a friend to me,' he said, finally, realising the words themselves were inadequate. They didn't feel enough, but he'd never been good at expressing himself because he'd never been allowed to.

'It's okay, Nate! I understand. You lost your parents…you had to be there for Lucas. I get it!' she said, cradling his face with her soft, gentle hand.

He leaned into it and closed his eyes at her touch and, when he opened them again, he realised that she was looking at him with such love and such yearning that he couldn't help what happened next.

Nate gazed at her for a moment and then he pulled her close, her body to his, feeling everything come alive at the feel of her against him, at the look in her eyes, knowing he would find the strength to let her go if she stopped this.

But she didn't stop him. She kissed him! And he let go of all the torment and allowed her kiss to whisk him away to another world.

Maddy wasn't sure how they made it back to her cabin. It was all a bit of a blur up on deck, a frenzy of need, when the kissing had made them both hungry for more. They'd both realised that out on the open deck, beneath the stars, was not the perfect place for them to sate the desires they both felt, however romantic. For that, they needed privacy. There was a brief memory of walking through the crew corridor as if everything was normal, a blurry image of her fumbling for her key card and then…

And then *everything.*

Clothes were pulled at and removed. Hands went on skin, desperate, hot, fevered. She was kissing him, fumbling with his belt buckle, falling backwards onto her bed. There was laughter, then the feel of his hot lips, his tongue upon her. She kicked off her shoes, struggling with a zip—'Just rip it, I don't care!'—and then…came the heat of him. Bare flesh pressed against her, solid muscle, hardness. She gasped for breath in between every lick, every bite, every kiss. She felt him sliding into her and arched her back, hands grasping, pulling him closer, urging him on, needing, needing, needing *more*…

‘Faster. Harder. Like that. *Oh, yes...*’

She felt his lips on her neck. Heat grew within her chest and she wanted just to lie there and absorb everything he could give, but she didn’t want it over just yet. It was too soon, so she rolled him over onto his back and then straddled him, her long hair swaying forward over her bare flesh, tickling at his nipples; she rode him, controlling the movement, slowing it down, rolling her hips as he reached for her breasts and told her she was beautiful.

She felt beautiful then. Felt *strong*. Felt all her feminine power as she smiled deliciously at him, and teasingly rocked her hips from back to front as he lay there, breathless, admiring her. Then before she knew it he’d rolled her onto her back and pinned her, arms above her head, slowly controlling the rhythm, grinning, kissing her neck and trailing his lips up its length to find her mouth, before he began to thrust hard again, grinding down against her, long and so deep, it almost hurt.

Almost.

As he thrust, she could feel her orgasm building. ‘Keep doing that…yes,’ she breathed, arching to meet every grind, every delightful movement that brought that orgasm closer and closer.

Had it been like that before? She couldn't remember. Did it even matter? She didn't care. Not in that moment; not in that heavenly moment as her breathing increased, they both got louder and then…her very soul seemed to explode as she came, Nate coming seconds later, riding the wave of her orgasm with his own.

And then everything slowed and time returned, reality coming back. The real world reinvited itself back into their lives.

Someone banged on the wall from the cabin next door and said, 'Nice finish! Well done! Can I get some bloody sleep now?'

Maddy looked up at Nate and they both laughed, before he collapsed into the bed next to her and held her close. And she knew that this time it was different, and this time she would never let him go.

CHAPTER SEVEN

HE SHOULD HAVE slept well but didn't, and the more he lay there with Maddy softly sleeping in his arms, the more guilty he felt. Had he used her for sexual gratification, knowing that he should never have let this get this far?

He didn't want to use her. Didn't want her to think that once he'd got what he wanted, what he needed, then he would walk away from her again. Because he didn't want to do that. If anything, he wanted to stay! And he would, but… what if he wasn't enough for her? What if he hurt her again? They worked together on a boat, for crying out loud. If this went wrong there would be nowhere for either of them to hide, and then she would leave. She would be the one walking away and he would never see her again.

He needed to be able to tell her the truth, to establish the parameters of this, the way they had before, but once he did she would look at him with disappointment and he couldn't do that. So, as he lay there with her in his arms, he told himself he would just pretend that everything was perfect, so that she wouldn't run for the hills when she found out the truth about Lucas. She wouldn't ruin his brother's big day and she wouldn't be mad at *him*.

He still doubted that he was good enough for her, so if he just kept it in the forefront of his mind that this was as before—friends with benefits—then he could hold back his heart from getting hurt, if it all went wrong. Because, if he was honest with himself, it had been easy to put Lucas's happiness and wellbeing first in everything because then he hadn't had to examine his own self-worth for too long.

Maddy stirred slightly and he nuzzled into her hair, inhaling her scent. He couldn't get enough of it. He couldn't get enough of her and he told himself that, if he soaked her all in, then if it did all go wrong, this time he would remember these sorts of moments, because before he'd thought nothing would come along to ruin it. It was simple. It was no-strings. They could do what they did guilt-free, because she wouldn't want anything from him, like a commitment. But this time he knew the risk of it going wrong, of losing her again. And that terrified him, because he knew his feelings for her were strong and getting stronger with every day.

'Morning,' she said, sleepy and happy.

'Morning.'

She turned in his arms to face him, tantalising him as she pressed her body even closer to his. He felt himself stir, and couldn't resist putting his fingers into her hair and pulling her close for an early-morning kiss.

'Sleep well?' he asked.

'Like a baby. You?'

'Same,' he said, lying, but knowing that he couldn't tell her that he'd lain there all night worrying about this going wrong again. But how could he not worry? Every relationship he had ever had with anyone had gone wrong. Life had been great with his mum until Bill had come along and then they'd become estranged. He'd loved his baby brother, until that relationship had become strained. Any time he'd been with a woman during his university years, it had been a one-off, and he'd quickly earned a reputation among the female students that he was not someone to go with if they wanted someone who would be there for them.

And with Maddy, the first time round, he'd screwed that up, too. Bill was right: he wasn't good enough. He didn't have what it took to keep someone.

'What time is it?'

He sighed. 'Time for work—we've a crew

clinic in about an hour. I ought to go back to my cabin and have a shower before then.'

'You could shower here with me,' she said.

He could picture that, standing in the hot spray with her, their wet, soapy bodies entwined in the steam, hot kisses and slick flesh… 'Mmm, sounds wonderful, but if we do that I'd never leave the shower cubicle and neither would you. Best I leave now and see you later.'

She mock-pouted. 'Okay. One last kiss before you go?'

He pressed his lips to hers and, though his body had fully responded in desire, he knew he had to pull away. He did so with an agonised groan and turned away from her, pulling on his clothes and standing, buttoning up his shirt and watching her as she lay, half-naked except for a sheet on the bed, her red hair haphazardly spread across the pillow.

Once he thought he had everything, he smiled at her. 'I'll see you in an hour.'

'Yes, boss.' She smiled.

He smiled back and then he was gone, closing her door and hoping that he hadn't made the biggest mistake in the world.

It had been inevitable really, she thought as she headed into work, that she and Nate would end up back in each other's arms. She'd felt it from the first moment she had seen him again—a tension in the air, electricity, the kind felt before a big storm. She'd felt it instantly and they'd both been pulled towards that meeting between the sheets, like moths drawn to lanterns burning brightly, unable to help themselves, destined to turn towards that which attracted them. She'd tried to fight it, tried to turn away, but there was no fighting the inevitable. There was no fighting fate, or whatever she wanted to call it.

And now she was glad that they hadn't. Being with him again had reawakened her dormant body in ways that other men had never been able to do, because there had been one or two others after he'd left. There'd been a couple of one night stands, just to scratch an itch, to let out frustrations from the day when things had gone wrong and she'd searched for something for herself. Something to make herself feel better, but of course it never had. If anything, she'd always felt worse, so she'd stopped doing that. She'd practically been celibate for the last two years.

But with Nate, the world seemed brighter. The very air seemed fresher.

The boat was moored off the coast of Corsica and, as was usual on a port day, they held a longer crew clinic as most passengers would disembark to see the sights and explore.

Maddy walked into the clinic feeling all bright and breezy and picked up her first patient file. 'Marco Giordano?'

A young man wearing engineering overalls stood up.

'Come with me.' She led him to a cubicle and got him to sit down on one of the examination beds. 'How can I help you today?'

'Is my hand.' He held it out, palm upwards, towards the ceiling, flexing and unflexing his fingers. 'I'm getting the…how you say…needles and pins? I drop things. Drop my tools.'

She nodded. 'Okay and how long has this been happening?'

'A couple of weeks.'

Weeks? That wasn't good. 'Anything make it better?'

Marco shrugged. 'Sometimes rest, but when you engineer, you don't get much.'

'I guess not. Are you alright for me to touch and examine you?'

He nodded.

'Okay.' Maddy performed an examination of not just his hand, but his wrist and shoulder, checking for impingement, any pain or numbness. She got him to grip her fingers, to pull, to push and tested his strength and grip against his other hand to see if there were any anomalies. 'Well, that all seems normal. Can you press the backs of your hands together, wrists bent, and hold it for about a minute?'

He did so.

'Any tingling?'

'Yes.'

Maddy nodded. 'I think you have something called carpal tunnel. It's caused by pressure on a nerve in your wrist. It makes you feel pain or numbness in your fingers and hand, and it can cause weakness and the problems that you've been having. I'm going to suggest you wear a wrist splint for a while, see how you get on with that, and then we'll have you back in a week to see how you're getting on.'

'And if it worse?'

'There are lots of options. We could do steroid injections, pain medication, or some people have to have surgery, though your doctors would need to do an ultrasound first. Let's do the splint and see how you get on. How does that sound?'

'Good. I don't want surgery—I need to work.'

'Of course. I'll let your supervisor know what I've suggested as well, so that they are aware.'

'Thank you.'

'No problem. I'll just get you that splint.'

Maddy was really enjoying her work now on *Serendipity*. It had eased her back into medicine nicely and it felt good to feel confident about being with patients again. And everything was turning out great with Nate, too! Life was certainly looking up, at last.

There was a bounce to her step as she thought about how her life had changed. She'd been so scared to accept this job, wondering if it would be too much being away from her home, away from everything and everyone she knew, sailing the seas, seeing the world and seeing patients again after her attack… She had never been at sea and had no idea if she got seasick. And, if she didn't like it then she'd be stuck doing so for half a year!

But, fortunately, she loved it and Nate was here and everything was finally working out for them… Maybe she would get a happy ending in her life. She felt that she'd certainly earned it!

After she'd fixed the splint to Marco's wrist, she sent him on his way and typed her notes into the system. She'd just finished her call with her patient's supervisor when Nate appeared, carrying two mugs. 'Tea break?' he said, smiling.

She nodded, smiling back. 'Sounds perfect.'

Nate was feeling terribly conflicted—fearful, full of doubt. Yet also hopeful that maybe all his fears were not founded and that he and Maddy could be fine, even if he was still keeping his fears about himself and Lucas from her. ‘How’s your morning going?’

She smiled at him, her eyes full of mischief and sexual allure. ‘Well, it started great.’

Yes, it had. Waking up with her in his arms had felt like coming home. That he was back in the place he was always meant to have been. He’d missed her so much over the years! But he couldn’t trust what he was feeling. He wasn’t sure of anything any more. He wasn’t used to thinking about himself and what he wanted or needed.

‘After crew clinic, we’ve a couple of hours before the ship sets sail again. I wondered if you’d like to come and explore Corsica with me? Grab a bite to eat somewhere?’ He suggested it so that they didn’t end up back in one of their cabin’s. He didn’t want this to get too deep. Who knew what she was feeling? And he didn’t dare ask, because what if she thought this was something more and he had to tell her otherwise?

‘Sounds amazing! I’d love to.’

‘Perfect. I’ve one patient I need to see in their cabin and then I’ll be free. Dr Galanis and Dr Hicks will be on call whilst we’re away from the ship in case anything crops up in the meantime, so…pick you up at twelve?’

‘I’ll be waiting.’ She reached for his hand as

he stood and pulled him in for a long, hot kiss that stirred his loins and dizzied his senses as he inhaled her perfume and flashed back to last night.

How could he be so hungry for her and yet, at the same time, feel so cautious?

I just don't want to hurt her but I might.

No-one knew about Lucas's past here—that he'd been a drug addict. No-one knew about Nate's uncertainties. He'd never dated anyone on board, even though he'd received plenty of offers. If anything, he had a reputation for being standoffish. He wasn't even sure he knew how to be in a relationship any more.

Could he give Maddy what she needed, what she *deserved*? Because she deserved happiness. A guy that could give her everything: commitment and a family. She wanted to settle down. And she deserved truth and honesty from the man she was with and he couldn't be honest with her. He yearned to be. But, if he told her his fears, then she would pull away from him and he didn't want that either. He just needed to keep up the charade until after Lucas's big day. Because he wouldn't risk disrupting his brother's big day—not when he was so close to happiness and setting himself free to work on himself.

Because he knew he loved Maddy. Maybe he

always had. And the idea that he might be letting down the woman he loved pained him terribly. He wanted to give her his all, to be able to talk to her about anything, to tell her the truth of why he'd left all those years ago—and not just the sanitised version he'd given her.

But if he got it wrong, he could lose her…and he was terrified of that.

Because only love could cause the level of pain he anticipated, if it all went wrong and *she* walked away from *him*.

When clinic was over, they signed out and headed dockside in Ajaccio, the capital of Corsica. They were only a few minutes' walk from the old town and it felt good to have her walk by his side. He wanted to show her all the beauty of this place and give her good memories, so that if it did all go wrong she might look back and remember that once, they'd been great.

She slipped her hand into his, surprising him. She looked happy, carefree. Sunglasses held her hair back from her face on this beautifully warm day with clear blue skies.

Plane trees in rich greens juxtaposed beautifully against the daffodil-yellow houses as they walked the alleys and boulevards towards the market, and once there they soon lost themselves, tasting cheeses, delicatessen meats and locally made honey on soft, warm bread. It was a veritable delight to the tastebuds and he smiled when she spotted a stall selling sweet, anise-flavoured biscuits and bought a box, alongside a slim bottle of myrtle oil. Touristy gift acquired, they headed for a local restaurant with a patio to eat *al fresco*.

They were seated beneath a canopy of grape vines and ordered wild boar stew served with fries and green beans and gâteau à la Farine de Châtaigne, sweet chestnut cake that would be served with a vanilla-bean ice-cream. The food was delicious, of course delicious. But he enjoyed the company more.

Maddy leaned back in her chair, full and satisfied, smiling, eyes crinkling behind her sunglasses. 'I'm so glad I came on board. You know… I had reservations when I realised you were here. Things ended so abruptly before, but now, I'm so, so happy.' She leaned forward then and took hold of his hand. '*You* make me happy.'

He smiled, thrilled with the compliment. 'You make me happy, too.' He couldn't say anything else. He most definitely couldn't say *I love you* because that would pull her deeper into his life and then, when the truth came out, she'd be even more hurt that he'd kept things from her. He told himself he was protecting her by not saying it, when in reality he was really protecting himself. He reckoned that, by holding back, by not giving his all, he would stop her from falling in love with him, because if he knew she loved him and then walked away that would be the most terrible thing of all.

She glanced at her watch. 'Ship sails in an hour, we should get back soon. Even if right now I feel like I don't want to leave this beautiful place. I think it's my favourite port so far.'

'And there's still so much we didn't see—the cathedral, the citadel, the Parata peninsular…'

'We can do that next time the ship docks here.'

Her fingers were still entwined with his and he glanced down at them. They were long, elegant, a faint pink blush on them. He could imagine a ring on her left hand on her ring finger, shining with a large diamond, and then he pushed the thought from his mind. What was he doing, torturing himself; thinking of weddings simply because Lucas was getting married? 'Lucas will be married by then. Has he been in touch with you about a dress for the ceremony? It's soon.'

'There might have been one or two emails.' She smiled. 'There's a dress I'm going to be picking up when we dock in Nice. Lucas showed it to me.'

'Really? What's it like?'

'It's a surprise. I want you to see me in it for

the first time on the day Lucas marries. Your brother is very excited.'

'Who wouldn't be, to marry the love of their life?'

She smiled. 'I envy him his certainty.'

Nate frowned. 'You do?'

'Of course! To *know*, the way he does, that Carlos is the man he wants to spend the *rest of his life* with!' She shook her head in disbelief. 'I think that's amazing. I don't think I've ever felt so sure about someone the way he does.'

'How do you mean?'

She shrugged. 'I've always second-guessed everybody. They say the right things, give you all the great soundbites, but when it comes to it? People let you down. But Lucas doesn't think that. He knows that Carlos has his back and won't ever let him down, and that's a gift, a certainty, I wish I had.'

Was she fishing? Nate felt guilty because he knew he'd let her down, proving her point. She could probably never, ever truly trust him, even if she did say that he made her happy. Because, if she couldn't trust him fully, she could never love him.

He hated that his thoughts and worries about this kept going round and round his head. 'We should get back to the ship.' He paid the bill and then stood and, when they left the restaurant and headed back to *Serendipity,* they no longer held hands. Simply because he'd been reminded that, no matter how much he wanted to love her the way he did, she could never be his. She would never trust him, because she couldn't trust anyone, and when she discovered the truth he would reinforce the fact that he could never be trusted.

Maddy was confused as they headed back to the ship. They'd walked into Ajaccio hand in hand and she'd felt amazing—like everything was working out. They'd had a great time at the market, and walking around the old town, and then at dinner something had changed and she wasn't sure what. Suddenly Nate seemed to hold part of himself back. But what they had was all so new; she didn't want to ruin it by asking him what was wrong.

Being with him last night had been amazing. To sleep in his arms had been wonderful, and she'd woken this morning wondering if this could possibly be her future. That, despite him leaving in the past, she knew what had happened now and understood him leaving. But the pain she'd felt upon losing him was not something she wanted to experience again. So, rather than ask him if anything was wrong, she decided to ignore the warning in her gut that he might already be pulling away again and told herself to keep quiet. It was probably just anxiety because of what had gone before. *He wasn't really going to leave!* Not after the perfect night they'd shared.

'Got anything planned this evening?' she asked him, knowing they were both off-duty until tomorrow now.

'I've a meeting and then I'm going to see Lucas. Help him plan his stag do on board.'

'Of course. It's not long now, is it?'

'Couple of days.'

'Well if the stag is the night before, don't let him get too hungover. He's going to want to enjoy his day.'

'Oh, he won't be drinking.'

'No? Why?'

Nate paused, then laughed, as if caught out by something. 'He just…doesn't really like the taste of it. I think he wants a sort of sports night—do the climbing wall, the on-board surfing, that kind of thing. Can't do those if you're paralytic!'

'I guess not.' It made sense.

They signed back on board, swiping their ID cards, and then Nate planted a kiss upon her cheek and excused himself. 'Gotta prep for my meeting. I'll see you tomorrow morning at work?'

'Of course.' But as she watched him go that strange feeling she'd felt earlier came back. She felt like he was holding something of himself back—that she wasn't being told everything.

And he did that before, remember? said the insidious, tiny voice in her head that was slowly getting louder.

Madeline bit her lower lip and headed in the other direction towards her own cabin.

Maybe everything would seem brighter in the morning.

Halfway through her morning passenger clinic, a young woman arrived, supported by her best friend as she hobbled in, clearly unable to bear weight on one of her feet. She was wearing a white bikini and patterned sarong and her friend wore a red swimsuit with a towel wrapped around her midriff. Both had wet hair.

'I slipped on some water poolside.' The hobbling woman, whose name was Sarah, cried as she hopped onto an examination bed.

Madeline frowned, looking concerned. The ankle did look malformed, and to have got here from the pools with just the help of her friend was very impressive indeed. 'Let's get you some painkillers first, before I examine you. It's a clear dislocation and I need to give you an intra-muscular opioid injection of morphine.'

'Dislocated?' Sarah looked upset, wiping at tears on her face. 'This all just gets worse and worse! Am I going to have to leave the boat?'

'We need to get this x-rayed to ensure there aren't any fractures and, if there aren't, then we should be able to perform a reduction on board and keep you here, if there aren't any complications.'

Maddy checked and double-checked the dosage, before injecting the painkiller, then gave it a moment to take effect before putting on examination gloves and eyeing the injury. There was no skin break, thankfully, which would have made this more complicated, and no vascular compromise. Hopefully the x-ray would confirm she could do a simple reduction. 'You just slipped? You weren't dizzy beforehand?'

'No.' Sarah's friend, Anna, passed her a tissue as she continued to cry.

Maddy looked up at her friend to see if she would explain why Sarah was so upset. Maybe it was just the pain, or feeling that her holiday was ruined… 'You might be off your feet for a bit, but don't worry, you've not ruined your holiday.'

'It's not my holiday!' Sarah cried. 'It's my honeymoon.'

'Failed honeymoon,' Anna added.

As Maddy arranged the x-ray, manoeuvring

the portable machine over Sarah's foot to get a good angle, she frowned. '*Failed* honeymoon?' she asked.

Sarah put down her tissue and looked at Maddy with panda eyes. 'I was supposed to be married now to the man of my dreams and enjoying this honeymoon cruise with him! But the jerk let me down and never showed and, because I didn't want to lose my money, I came on my honeymoon with Anna!'

'Chief bridesmaid and best friend,' Anna added.

'Oh. I see. I'm sorry to hear that.' She carefully and gently placed the x-ray plate beneath Sarah's ankle and made final adjustments with the machine. 'Did he say why he didn't show?'

'Said he wasn't ready. That he couldn't give me what I needed. You'd think he'd have worked that out before the morning of the wedding!'

'Jerk,' agreed Anna, clearly no stranger to helping Sarah vent.

The x-rays confirmed no break and Maddy gave the good news to a rather resigned patient. 'I can do the reduction here. You won't have to leave the ship. But afterwards, I will have to immobilise the joint with a splint and take a final x-ray just to ensure everything is where it's meant to be, okay? And we'll book you in for a follow-up at a clinic in Nice.'

'Will it hurt?'

'I'll sedate you so you shouldn't remember it.'

'The ankle or my idiot of an ex-fiancé? I'm telling you, doc, don't ever fall in love. The cost is much too high to pay.'

Sarah was probably right. Look at how much her own feelings were being bounced around already with Nate and they weren't planning a wedding, she thought. Well, not their own, anyway. Love certainly didn't have a smooth path.

Was it meant to? Was love *meant* to be easy? Was that how she'd know for sure she was in love, because there weren't any problems? Because, if that was the case, then what did it say about Nate and her?

'Okay, I'm going to go and get someone to help me with this, and when I come back I'm going to sedate you, okay?'

Sarah nodded and dabbed at her eyes. 'Fine.'

Nate helped Maddy provide traction on an ankle reduction for a patient who had slipped by a pool. After examining the x-rays together afterwards, ensuring the joint was realigned, they placed the patient, Sarah, into a special supportive boot, gave her a set of crutches and told her to be careful.

'This was meant to be her honeymoon,'

Maddy said to him after their patient limped away, aided and abetted by her friend, Anna.

'Meant to be?'

'The groom was a no-show, so she's here on the cruise with her chief bridesmaid instead.'

'She got jilted at the altar? Poor girl. I can't even imagine.'

Maddy looked at him. 'I can. Imagine being so totally in love with someone and discovering the other person didn't feel the same way. Sarah must be in hell.'

Did she know? Or was she talking about before? She couldn't know his true feelings…

'Do you think you could ever imagine being in such a situation that you wouldn't show up to your own wedding?' she asked.

He thought about it for a moment. If the bride were Maddy, he couldn't imagine it. 'No. I mean I'd like to think that, if there were doubts or cold feet, I'd have the wherewithal to discuss those with the bride before it even got to that stage. In fact, if there were doubts, I don't think I'd have even proposed, never mind have got to the altar.' But it was easier said than done, wasn't it? Hypotheticals were all well and good, but when it came down to it no-one wanted to hurt another person intentionally. Not like that.

'So…logically then…if you had worries about us, reservations, you'd talk to me about them?'

'Of course.' He smiled, feeling his cheeks colour. Did she suspect he had reservations? He desperately wanted to be fully committed. He wanted just to take her by the hand and tell her that he loved her! He was holding back the truth about Lucas, because he had sworn him to secrecy. And because, if Maddy found out afterwards that she had been a bridesmaid for an addict, he didn't want her hating him.

No. It's easy to blame my reservations on that. It's me. I don't think I'm good enough for her. What if I'm not? 'But it's not like we're in something serious, right? We're just having fun.'

'Fun?' Her smile faltered and she distracted herself by putting things away, tidying up after herself in the small cubicle. 'Of course. It's not like we're committed; we've made no promises to one another.'

'Exactly.' He nodded, watching her busy herself, wishing with all his might that he could take hold of her, pull her close and say, 'I was lying just then. I want us to be more. I want us to be official.'

But he didn't. Fear kept the words and the desire to say them choked up in his throat. He cleared it and pushed the curtains of the cubicle open. 'Well, I'd better let you get on. Has Lucas told you yet about the wedding rehearsal?'

'No.'

'Tomorrow, in the Captain's lounge. Just so we all know where we'll be standing and what he needs us to do, is that okay? About three?'

Maddy nodded and gave him a bright smile. 'Fine!'

She was okay with it. *Cool.* 'Great. I'll see you later.'

CHAPTER EIGHT

It was lovely to see Lucas again. He was one of those people that just made Maddy smile to be with him. He was fun and outrageous and clearly the star of his own life, and right now he was the romantic lead. His love for Carlos and his eagerness to get married, on board in front of all of his friends, was beautiful and Maddy felt that she needed beauty right now with her heart being broken yet again by Nate.

They'd arrived in Nice that morning and Maddy had collected the bridesmaid dress that Lucas had approved. It was hanging in her cabin and she would not let anyone see it until the big day. It was an asymmetrical, off the shoulder, pale-green, floor-length, silky delight that showed off Maddy's red hair beautifully and she felt wonderful wearing it. Lucas had let her know that there would be a small floral hairpin for her to wear, as well as a small bouquet to hold. He had spent an hour with her in her cabin, discussing which shoes would go well with the dress and, as she didn't have anything suitable, they'd gone to the very expensive shop on *Serendipity*'s promenade and Lucas had paid for a beautiful heel, with a diamanté flourish on the side.

He wanted everything to be perfect. During the time she'd spent with him, she really felt she'd got to know him. Lucas was amazing and she couldn't wait to see him marry the love of his life.

'So you and Nate will go up the aisle first, starting here, okay?' Lucas drew an imaginary line. 'And where those chairs are, imagine the arch and where the captain will be waiting to perform the service.'

'The captain isn't part of the rehearsal?'

'He's done this before and, between you and me, he probably doesn't need an ice-dancer from his ship tell him what to do!' Lucas winked, positioning Maddy closer to Nate. 'You'll want to slip your arm into his or something. What's the matter with you two?'

'Nothing.' Maddy turned to face Nate and smiled, before sliding her arm into his and facing forward.

'And play the music.'

The Captain's lounge filled with a piece of soft, classical music, a known love ballad.

'And walk.'

Lucas stood in front of them, backing away, smiling broadly as she and Nate began their slow walk up the aisle.

Maddy reminded herself quite strongly as she did so that she and Nate were just bridesmaid and best man and would never be the bride and groom. But she couldn't help herself. It was almost impossible not to think about it!

Ever since she'd been a little girl, alone in her communal room, she had imagined the day she might get married. She'd pulled a pillowcase from her pillow and draped it over her head for a veil. She's scrunched up a floral print top and pretended it was her bouquet, and imagined walking up an aisle, knowing that all eyes were on her. The eyes of loved ones, of friends who loved her: co-workers, besties. They would all gaze upon her and think her the most beautiful bride in the world! And then she would get to the end of the aisle and there would be the man of her dreams.

When she'd been a child, the groom's face had always been a blur, but she'd known that he loved her more than he loved life itself. That she would forever be his princess, his queen, his bride and best friend…and he would *love* her.

As a child, she'd not really known what love felt like and it had been something she had chased for a long time. And then, when she'd got it, she'd not realised just how much pain it would cause her when the man she loved disappeared without a word. The man who now held her arm in his as they reached the end of the aisle.

'Bellissima!' Lucas clapped, beaming, placing a head on Carlos's shoulder before turning to his husband-to-be, holding his hands and gazing into his eyes.

They went through the whole imagined ceremony, practising it a couple of times over, Lucas explaining in great detail what would be happening to ensure that not a single thing went wrong. When it was over, Maddy and Nate headed back to the medical clinic.

'It's going to be a lovely wedding,' Maddy said conversationally.

'Yes. I can officially sign off care of my brother to someone else.'

'And then what will you do with all that free time?'

Nate laughed. 'Oh, I don't know…take off somewhere? Go explore the Sahara or trek across the Arctic?'

Was that a joke answer because he didn't know what he was going to do? Or was it a real one, to let her know that, in all likelihood, he was going to take off again? The idea that he might disappear on her *again* sullied the day.

'Well, I'll miss you, if you do,' she said. 'But you must do what's right for you. After all, you did go running the second he needed you, so I guess your life will become your own to do with how you please.'

She would miss him, terribly, but she would not let it show. Would not let him see that he had made a fool of her again. He did not deserve that power. If he did think they were just friends with benefits, then friends with benefits they would be!

'Just let me know before you go this time,' she said, pushing open the door to the bathroom and disappearing inside just as the pain of her tears hit her eyes. She would not cry over this man again!

'Damn it!' she swore softly to herself as she stood in front of the mirror, dabbing at her eyes with a blue paper-towel from the dispenser. Why had she let herself hope that, because they'd slept with each other again, they were something more? That they were *involved*, in a *relationship*. He'd made no such declaration and nor had she asked him. *I should have set out the intentions from the start!* Only she'd not, because she'd been busy tearing off his clothes, seeking out his skin and giving in to the lust that had been building.

When will I ever learn when it comes to him?

* * *

Well I'll miss you, if you do.

He'd made some off-hand comment about exploring some far-off remote places once Lucas was married, but only because each time he'd walked her down that pretend aisle in the Captain's lounge, he'd thought about how it might feel to see Maddy in a beautiful white dress, walking up the aisle *to him.*

He could imagine himself marrying Madeline, and that terrified him, because that meant his feelings for her ran so deep he was imagining for ever with her and that meant he was getting hopeful. That he was making plans. But he was so terrified of not being good enough for her; having broken her heart once already, he was terrified of doing so again. What if he got this part wrong, or the next part? It could all fall apart so quickly and he didn't want to lose her. And she would clearly miss him if he did decide to take off and get some space for himself, because when was the last time he'd actually been by himself?

In his first job at London Saint, he'd had Maddy, and then he'd come rushing home at the news of their parents' death and Lucas's overdose and he'd been with his brother. He'd been with him intensively these last few years, watching him get sober, helping him recover, encouraging him to build the life for himself that had always been denied him. And then, when Lucas had got the job on board the cruise ship and had been nervous about what would happen if he lost his brother, his support system by his side, Nate had got a job on board too. To be there. Backup. Just in case. They had been on many different ships together.

Now Lucas was going to marry Carlos and it would set Nate free—but he wasn't sure *how* to be free. Who would he be without his brother to need him? Nate had never been by himself and maybe he needed that space to know what he wanted for sure, whether he wanted a full-on relationship with Maddy or not. So, yes, he'd suggested he explore the Sahara or the Arctic, be by himself and sort out his feelings, because being this close to her was scrambling his brain, and sometimes he didn't know which way was up. One inner voice told him just to be with her and another told him that he would just hurt her again.

I don't want to hurt her.

Could he really walk away and take some time for himself? Maddy said she'd miss him, but he knew for sure that, if he did, when he came back the door to them being a thing would be closed—permanently. No, he had to decide before then if he was good enough.

Maybe I should ask Lucas if I can tell her about his addiction. That way, he'd be telling her the whole truth about why he'd left, but then he'd hurt Lucas by bringing up a past he had worked so hard to put behind him. His brother would always be an addict, but he'd been sober for years and, with the exception of Carlos and him, no-one knew about it. His brother would not want to be thought of differently, lose friends or have someone think they could tempt him back with something.

He felt stuck between a rock and a hard place.

Nate picked up a patient admission file. A woman, aged thirty-six, had come to the medical bay with intense back and hip pain. The file said she was struggling to walk. At least he could help his patients, even if he couldn't find the right path to help himself and free himself of all the turmoil he felt.

'Marissa?' A woman in the waiting area, sitting with a man holding her hand, stood with difficulty, wincing slightly as they made their way over to him.

'Let's get you to a cubicle,' he said, guiding her and slowing his pace as she ambled along behind him. 'I'm Dr Blake and you are…?'

'Mason. I'm her husband.'

'Nice to meet you both. Okay, Marissa, what's

the most comfortable position for you? Sitting? Standing? Lying down?'

'Can I just lie down for a moment please?' She sounded a little breathless.

'Sure thing.' Her husband helped her up, and she winced and groaned as she settled herself with some relief onto the examination bed. 'So, tell me what's been happening.'

Marissa shook her head as if she couldn't quite explain, or understand what was happening. 'I don't know. Everything's been fine. I'm usually in good health and I don't usually suffer with my back or anything like that.'

'She does yoga, pilates. She's always been fit,' her husband added.

'Have you done anything recently that might contribute to this back pain?'

'We did the climbing wall yesterday and I was in a harness. Could I have stretched funny, do you think?'

'Possibly. On holiday people try a lot of new things they don't normally do and using different sets of muscles can trigger a problem. If you had to rate the pain from zero to ten, with zero being no pain and ten being the worst pain you've ever felt in your life, how would you rate it?'

'It's hard to say…it seems to come in waves and, when it does, I'd put it at maybe a six or a seven. Oh, it's coming now…' Marissa groaned and scrunched up her face as she dealt with the pain.

Nate grabbed a blood-pressure cuff, which he placed around her upper arm, and a SAT monitor, which he placed on her finger. Her blood pressure was slightly elevated, which was no doubt from the pain, and her pulse was slightly high too, but her oxygen SATs were normal. 'Does the pain come and go like this all the time? When did it start?'

When she could breathe again, she nodded. 'Yes. It started this morning. I woke at about four. I figured it was muscular, took a painkiller and went back to sleep, but the tablet did nothing and it kept waking me up.'

'I'll just take your temperature.' He placed the electronic thermometer in her ear, but her temperature was normal. 'Eating and drinking okay?'

'I felt a little nauseous earlier, but I had my breakfast.'

'Toileting okay? No diarrhoea?'

'I did have some cramps and had a bowel movement, but no diarrhoea.'

'And when was your last menstrual period?'

'Two weeks ago.'

'And they've been normal lately?'

Marissa nodded. 'Yes.'

'What do you think it is, doc?' Mason asked.

'Could be any number of things. Can you roll onto your side so I can examine your back? I'll feel down your spine and you tell me when and where it hurts, okay?'

'Okay.'

He palpated her vertebrae, starting at her neck and moving down to her lower sacrum, where Marissa indicated it was sore. 'And, when the pain comes, what does it feel like? Is it burning? Sharp? Dull?'

'I don't know how to describe it, except to say it's powerful and comes in waves.'

'Any pattern to these waves?'

Marissa and Mason both shrugged. 'We weren't timing them, so don't have a clue.'

'Could I examine your abdomen, would that be alright?'

'Fine.' Marissa manoeuvred herself into place and lifted her top.

Her stomach looked unremarkable, but when he palpated he could feel a mass…a mass that felt remarkably ominous. But he kept his expression blank and told her she could lower her top. 'I'd like to do an ultrasound and maybe bring in a colleague. I won't be a moment.'

'What's wrong? Did you feel something?' Mason asked.

'I'll be back in a moment.' Nate pulled the cubicle curtain across and let out a breath, then he went looking for Maddy. He reckoned he would need her for what he suspected was coming next. He found her in one of the utility rooms. 'Got a sec?'

She nodded. 'Sure. What's up?'

'I need your help with a patient, who I strongly suspect may be in labour with a cryptic pregnancy.' A cryptic pregnancy was a pregnancy which passed by the full nine months completely undetected by medical professionals or the mother herself.

'You're joking!'

'No. She's having what I think are contractions, even though her belly is flat. She's been having periods, but when I palpated her abdomen I could feel what felt like a term baby. I'm going to ultrasound her, but if we've got a labouring mother on board she might prefer a female doctor, so thought I'd get you to co-consult and then, if she wants you to take over her delivery, you'll know each other.'

'Wow. Okay. I've never seen one of these before. You?'

'No. Never. And I've not told them of my suspicions yet. I thought I'd do the ultrasound first to confirm and then tell them.'

'Okay. You're the boss.'

He nodded. Yes, he was, and he had that to

think of too. There were thousands of people on this ship who depended on having a good team there for them any hour of any day of their cruise. He wanted Maddy to feel wanted, needed, even if he couldn't give her everything he wanted to.

When they got back to the cubicle, he pushed the ultrasound machine in and began to set it up, whilst introducing Maddy.

Marissa experienced another wave of pain and, timing it surreptitiously, Nate noted that it was almost a minute long. If he was right, her pains were going to get a lot more frequent and a lot more powerful.

'Now, Marissa, I'm just going to squirt this gel onto your abdomen; it can feel cold, okay?' Her belly was so flat! It was hard to believe that there was a baby tucked away in there.

'Okay,' she breathed, coming down from the pain.

Mason reached for her hand and held it with both of his.

Nate was glad that Marissa had her husband as support, because he suspected they were both about to have the surprise of their lives. He placed the transducer wand onto Marissa's belly, smearing the gel widely, and then began to focus his attention on what could be seen on the screen. He had it angled towards himself and Maddy, who stood behind him, watching closely.

And he'd guessed correctly. Marissa was pregnant to term! The baby measured at thirty-nine weeks and six days.

Nate turned to glance at Maddy and they both nodded to one another.

'What is it? What do you see?' Marissa asked.

'This isn't easy to say and it's going to be a shock.' Nate reached for the screen and turned it round. 'The pains you are having are contractions and you are about to give birth to a full-term baby.'

There was a moment of thick, stunned silence as Marissa and Mason stared hard at the screen. There was their baby, clear as day.

'Pregnant?' Mason said.

Marissa shook her head in denial. 'But… I've been having periods! It's got to be wrong!'

'It's not wrong. The measurements indicate a nearly forty-week baby. Your periods were probably breakthrough bleeds—it happens sometimes in what we call cryptic pregnancies.'

'I can't be pregnant! Not full term!' Marissa cried, then winced as another contraction hit.

It did not escape Nate's notice that Mason had pulled his hand free from his wife's. A moment ago, they had been united by her pain, and he had seemed supportive and loving. Now, Mason looked shocked and—if Nate had to guess—angry.

'We've only been back together for four months, so…whose is it?' Mason asked his wife.

Nate did not expect that. He wiped the gel from Marissa's belly and when her contraction was over and said, 'We'll give you a moment alone, but Marissa, you're in labour and we'll need to get you on some foetal monitoring. I'm assuming you've had no pre-natal care.'

Marissa began to cry.

Mason stood staring at her, as if he didn't recognise her.

Nate and Maddy left the cubicle.

'We need to get her in a private room,' Maddy said.

'We will, but let's just give them a minute. They've had a shock.' Nate and Maddy walked over to the reception desk.

From where they stood, they could hear the argument.

'You lied to me!'

'You never told me the truth, ever!'

'How will I ever trust you?'

Mason was shouting…a lot.

'We should go back,' Nate said. 'She doesn't need this right now.'

'Maybe not, but he's asked a valid question. Trust is everything and if you feel like someone is lying to you, or you know that they are, it can ruin everything.'

The way she's looking at me... 'Maddy, I really don't think that now is the time.'

'It never is with you.'

But there was no time for them to discuss it, or for him to ask what she meant. *'Dr Finch...'* He reined in his anger. He'd tried, he'd tried so hard, but this was what he did! This was what he was trying to protect her from! Could she not see that he was protecting her? 'Let's go tend to our patient. Mason can get his answers after we make sure mum and baby are okay. Can we get the captain notified of the imminent delivery in case we need to get them both airlifted out of here?' He gave instructions.

Maddy blanched and picked up the phone as he headed back to the cubicle with a wheelchair, so that he could wheel Marissa to a private room for the delivery.

They had all they needed to deliver a baby, but if the baby needed support afterwards, or there were complications with the delivery and it became an emergency situation, Nate would prefer Marissa and her baby to be in a facility fully equipped to deal with such a situation.

Mason followed forlornly as Nate wheeled his patient to a private room and got her onto a bed.

Maddy followed a moment or so after. 'The captain is going to divert to the closest port just in case, and an obstetrician is going to be on standby to receive them. Dr Ottilie is available to virtually assist, if we need it.' Her tone was curt.

'Thank you.' She was pulling away. He'd hurt her again. He knew it. But there was no time for him to address it. Marissa and her baby were the priority here. 'Marissa, as you're in labour, we're going to need to examine you internally, see how you're progressing. Either myself or Dr Finch could do it. Do you have a preference?'

'Dr Finch.'

'Maddy?' He turned to her. She was already washing her hands and preparing to put on gloves. 'I'll get the CTG machine so we can keep an eye on baby and your contractions as you progress.'

He'd only ever had to use the machine once before on a cruise. Venture Line Cruises had a ruling that no one was allowed to sail after the twenty-third week of pregnancy, and anyone sailing before that had to have a letter from their doctor confirming that they were low risk and healthy to board. But there'd been one poor lady who started contracting in her twenty-first week and the ship had been so far from a port that she'd been airlifted off. Thankfully, the hospital she'd ended up at had managed to stop her contractions. He'd never had to use it on a woman at term before.

'Okay, try to relax,' Maddy said as she performed the internal examination. 'You're at seven centimetres, you're moving fast!' She sounded impressed.

Marissa let out a moan of fear and grasped for her husband's hand.

Nate could see by the look on the man's face that he was torn. Clearly they'd had a tumultuous relationship, from what he could tell a break-up and then a reconnection, and in that time his wife had slept with someone else and not told him. Now he was having to deal with the fact that the woman he loved was about to give birth to someone else's baby.

He couldn't imagine how that felt. The idea that Maddy might find a haven in another man's arms… Would he have been able to do it? Would he have been able to forgive her?

'Oh God, here comes another one!'

'Marissa, would you like some gas and air? We have Entonox on board,' Maddy said.

Marissa nodded frantically, her hands gripping the mattress as she contorted and tried to breathe through the strengthening contractions.

We're going to deliver this baby. It's coming fast. His mind went into automatic mode. All other thoughts, all other concerns about himself, Lucas and Maddy, went out of the window.

Her waters suddenly broke and thankfully they were clear. Even though he knew this was happening, knew that he'd seen a term baby on the ultrasound, there was still an element of disbelief about the whole thing, because Marissa didn't look pregnant. She looked three or four months' pregnant, nothing more. Her belly was gently rounded like any woman's, but nothing that screamed advanced pregnancy.

'Oh God, I want to push!' Marissa screamed.

'Try to breathe through it. I need to check you,' Maddy said.

He and Maddy moved perfectly as a team. Just like the good old days when they used to surround a new incoming patient to A&E, assessing, checking and working together to ensure the safety and health priorities of their patient. It was like a dance. Perfectly coordinated, they began to coach Marissa through pushing as, unbelievably, she was fully dilated.

Marissa sucked in breaths and began to push.

By Nate's estimate from the ultrasound, the baby was nearly seven pounds—a good weight, a healthy weight. He could only pray that, when it was born, the baby would be able to breathe on its own and not need any assistance. He'd not seen anything of concern on the scan, which was good news, but he could never know for sure.

'And push again, Marissa! Just like that! Perfect!' Maddy coached.

The head was beginning to crown. The baby had thick, black hair, just like its mother.

'I don't think I can do this! We don't have anything! We're not prepared! You hate me!' Marissa cried.

'I don't hate you,' Mason said. 'I love you. We can work this out, but not if you don't push!'

Nate looked at him, surprised, but glad that he was choosing to support his wife, despite all he'd had to take in during the last hour: that his wife's back pain wasn't from rock-climbing; that she was pregnant; that she was full term. That she was in labour and that the baby she was delivering was not his. But he was there for her. It gave him hope that maybe things would turn out just as well for Maddy and him.

'Okay, on the next contraction, the baby's head will crown and I'll tell you when to stop pushing and when to just breathe it out and let it come nicely so you don't tear, okay?'

Marissa nodded, then sucked in another breath and began to push with all her might.

The head slowly emerged and, just as it got to the widest part, Maddy instructed Marissa to stop pushing and let the head crown by itself. 'Just breathe…that's it…you're doing great. Okay, head's out! Do you want to touch your baby?'

Marissa reached down. 'Oh!' She smiled and laughed, her head flopping back onto the pillow.

'Next contraction is the shoulders and your baby will be here in no time.'

Nate gathered the towels and blankets that he'd taken from the cupboards, ready to wrap the baby. He also had scissors for the cord, and a clamp that he'd thought he'd never have to use, but which they had in stock just in case of emergencies such as this one.

Marissa pushed and Maddy caught the baby as it slithered out and instantly began to cry as she placed the baby on Marissa's chest and into her waiting hands.

Marissa and Mason were crying.

Nate placed the towels around the baby, drying it, keeping it warm, whilst Maddy dealt with the afterbirth and checked Marissa for tears.

'Just a first-degree tear there, Marissa, but that should heal on its own. You did good!' Maddy said.

Nate knew the sex of the baby. He'd seen it during the delivery and on the scan. 'Know what you've got yet?'

Marissa looked, then gasped with delight. 'It's a boy!'

Once everybody was cleaned up, Nate and Maddy left Marissa and Mason to bond as a family. Nate informed the captain that the baby had been born and everything was well. The ship would still sail into Cannes and offload mum and baby for a proper check-up by Dr Ottilie, an obstetrician.

'Never thought I'd do that,' Nate said as Maddy brought him a cup of tea afterwards.

'Nor me. But life always likes to throw you little surprises.'

'It certainly does,' he said, thinking back to how he'd felt when he'd learned that Maddy would be joining his ship as a doctor—a woman he'd never thought he would see again.

'Do you think they'll be alright?' Maddy asked.

'Marissa and Mason?'

She nodded.

'I hope so. If they can get through that, they can get through anything.'

Maddy went silent for a moment, staring at her cup in her hands, then she lifted her head and looked directly at him. 'I know what it feels like to realise that the person you love is withholding something from you.'

His heart began to pound. She *loved* him!

'I know that you're keeping yourself held back but I don't know why. I don't understand why you aren't able to commit to me, when clearly there's something powerfully strong between us.'

'Maddy—'

'Do you not love me? Is that it? Am I not worthy of you loving me? Because that's how it feels, and I don't want to continue this contract on this ship knowing that I want to give you all of my love, but you can't do the same.'

He felt lost for words. He wanted to explain, but was not sure that he was able. She was asking him perfectly reasonable questions! So why did his throat feel as if it had seized up?

'Have I read too much into what we have? Is that it? Have I fallen back into old behaviours and hopes and given my heart to the *idea of us*, when there is no *us*?'

Maddy stared at him, waiting for an answer. Why couldn't he just put her out of her misery? Tell her straight? He looked uncomfortable at her questions, at her declaration of loving him. *Oh God, why did I tell him that I love him?*

She felt embarrassed, humiliated, especially if it wasn't reciprocated.

He kept opening his mouth, as if he was about to speak, but no words emerged for a moment, then he said, 'You deserve someone who can give you *all* of their heart. All of their love.'

'And?' She stared at him. 'You can't?'

'I could, but…you deserve someone better than me. Someone who hasn't hurt you. Someone who hasn't let you down.'

'You let me down when you don't communicate. When you hold something back of yourself. What are you holding back? What aren't you telling me? You should trust me. Don't you trust me?'

'Of course I do!'

'So why won't you tell me what's wrong?'

He didn't answer. And that in itself was an answer.

She stood, unable to be in the small room with him a moment longer. 'I'm going to check on the baby.'

Upset, disappointment and hurt filled her heart as she walked away, unable to believe why he couldn't give her an answer. Why he couldn't even explain to her why he held back part of himself. If anyone should hold themselves back it ought to be her! She was the one who had been hurt by him before. She was the one who had been let down!

Maddy had never let *him* down. So why did he not give her all of himself?

It's always been complicated with him! I should know this.

She rapped her knuckles softly against Marissa's door and entered, forcing a smile. 'How are we all doing?'

'We're good,' Marissa said, smiling, her arms filled with her son, still wrapped in a blanket.

'We'll arrive in port soon. We'll get you seen by specialists and maybe give you the opportunity to get some baby things.'

'My family are going to be so surprised. You expect to come back from a holiday with a tan, not a baby.'

'Have you thought of a name yet?'

'I like Elliot. Or Jacob. I haven't decided.'

'How about you, Mason?' Maddy asked.

'It should be Marissa's decision. It's her baby.'

His wife turned to him. 'It's our decision. I'd like your input. I'd like to know what you're thinking.'

'My opinion is important?'

'Yes! I didn't plan this, Mason! It happened to me too, but we both need to be grown-up about it and talk to one another if we're going to get through this. This should be a happy day for us. We always said we wanted to try for a family and, like it or not, we've now got one, so what are you going to do about it?'

'I'll leave you to it. Would you like a cup of tea? Something to eat? I could get the kitchen to bring you both something down,' Maddy suggested.

Marissa nodded. 'Thank you.'

Maddy closed the door and sighed. It looked as if they were having communication issues too. But Marissa was right, they would have to communicate to get through it, just as she and Nate ought to. She knew she'd need to talk to him before the wedding, but right now she needed space from him because it would be no good talking to him whilst she was still angry.

Nate would have to wait for her for a change.

CHAPTER NINE

THE CAPTAIN'S LOUNGE had been transformed for the wedding ceremony. Chairs for the guests sat in neat lines, each one adorned with a small posy of flowers in the heart of a pale-green ribbon. An arch of fresh flowers sat at the end of the aisle and flower petals covered the floor. Captain Thomas stood beneath the arch, resplendent in his finest uniform, waiting for the two grooms.

Maddy had felt apprehensive dressing in her bridesmaid's dress. She'd meant to find Nate and talk to him about their argument yesterday, to clear the air, at least for the wedding. But she'd gone to her cabin and fallen asleep almost instantly, exhausted by the day and her emotions, and now it was too late. But for the sake of Lucas and Carlos, who deserved nothing but happiness on their special day, she would not give them any reason to think that there were hostilities between Nate and her. It would be difficult, but she would do it.

A beautician from the ship's spa had done her hair and make-up. Maddy had sat in the chair, looked at her pale face and watched as the beautician had created a miracle of healthy glow upon her skin. She'd put soft curls into Maddy's hair and pinned them with flowers and now she was ready.

She saw Lucas and Carlos separately before the service, gave each of them a kiss and wished them both the best. Then, before she knew it, the music began and Nate was there. He looked stunning in a dinner suit and he held out his arm for her to take to walk up the aisle together in time to the music, as they'd practised.

She gave Nate a polite smile, wishing so much that things were different, and began her way up the aisle with him.

Everyone was looking at them: all of Lucas's and Carlos's friends and colleagues who had been invited and the captain. She could feel her heart pounding in her chest, and it felt as if it would burst out of her ribcage at any moment. Nate's reassuring arm held her upright and she felt him look at her as they glided up the aisle to their positions.

Strange to think that she'd once imagined walking up the aisle with Nate. But not like this.

Looks like I never will either.

The thought saddened her so powerfully in that moment that she felt herself gulp and force back tears, but it was fine, because she knew everyone would just think that she was trying to hold back her joy for the happy couple about to come up the aisle themselves.

Maddy pulled her arm free to take her place but, unexpectedly, Nate took her hand, brought it up to his lips and kissed it, his gaze never leaving hers. Breathless, she stared at him, wondering what it meant, but unable to ask, because at that moment the music changed and Carlos walked up the aisle.

Maddy turned away from Nate, bewildered, confused, forcing a wide smile back onto her face as Carlos came to stand in front of the captain. Carlos wore a pale-cream suit, with a tie the same colour as her dress, and a buttonhole of a white rose and pale-green eucalyptus. Carlos met her gaze and beamed at her before turning to look back down the aisle as Lucas appeared.

With no parent to walk him up the aisle, all he had was his brother. Nate now walked back down the aisle and offered his arm to his brother, surprising him.

Lucas pressed his hand to his heart, looking incredibly touched, and together they walked up the aisle, Lucas looking resplendent in his own off-white suit. At the end of the aisle, Nate and his brother embraced, then he took his brother's hand and placed it in Carlos's, before stepping back.

Maddy could not take her eyes off Nate during the service. She could see that his eyes were full of love for his brother and she knew that he would give his life for his brother. That he would do nothing that would make him turn away from him. That they knew absolutely everything about one another and still loved each other fiercely. That patient, Mr Stanton, had been wrong about Nate. There'd been problems, but he'd never abandoned his brother, and he could be trusted.

If only he could feel that way about me.

The tears in her eyes were as much for her as they were for the happy couple and she wasn't too aware of the words being exchanged, or the vows said. Her own heart was breaking as theirs were joining in matrimony. She managed to pull herself together for the rings, though, the captain announcing them as husband and husband and the kiss they shared. Then, before she knew it, Nate was there again, offering her his arm as they followed the happy couple back down the aisle and off to the reception.

There was a whirlwind of greeting people

as they entered. and the meal was a blur of courses that she picked at, unable to eat, then there were speeches to listen to, dances to watch and then finally…*finally*...she could slip away, stand under the stars on the top deck and simply *breathe*.

She felt as if she could hear her own heart beating. That her own heart was trying bravely to carry on, despite having broken, but then she became aware of someone standing behind her and knew who it was.

'Maddy…are you alright?' It was Nate.

She turned to face him, appalled that she still found him handsome. She still found him incredibly attractive, especially now that he'd pulled off the bow-tie, which hung undone around the collar of his opened shirt. 'I will be.'

'It was a good service.'

She nodded. 'It was.' What she could remember of it. 'You disappeared after the meal. I thought maybe you didn't want to see me.'

'I wanted to see you very much. I wanted to put everything right between us, but there was someone I needed to speak to first before I could.'

Maddy frowned. What was he talking about? 'Who?'

'Lucas.'

Now she was even more confused. 'Why?'

Nate came to stand by her side, reaching to take her hand. 'You asked me before about why I was holding a part of myself back and I couldn't tell you—partly, because I'd made a promise to my brother long ago, but also because I didn't feel worthy of you.'

How did a long-ago promise to his brother have anything to do with them? 'I don't understand.'

'I told you about our parents.'

She nodded.

'We did not have the best relationship. My stepfather, Bill, hated me. Made me feel all my life like I was nothing, not worthy enough of his time or attention or love. He put me down at every opportunity and favoured Lucas. It soured everything and I left as quickly as I could. I figured Lucas would be fine. Bill was his real father and Bill loved his son. At least, until Lucas came out as gay, then that changed too.'

Maddy stared at him, wrapped up in the pain of his story.

'I hadn't spoken to my family, or my brother, for years when you knew me, when we first got together. I kept you at a distance because I honestly believed I wasn't good enough for anything else. That I didn't know how to commit, or what love truly was, and that I was probably bad. So I held you at arm's length, not realising the depth of your feelings. At the same time, Lucas had…well…he had come out and been rejected and he…he succumbed to the temptations of drugs to block out the pain he felt.'

'Drugs? He was a drug addict?' Now she began to see. To *understand.*

He doesn't take painkillers.

He doesn't drink.

Flashbacks to being attacked by the drug addict flooded her mind and she grew hot and uncomfortable. Struggling to reconcile her feelings for the event that had given her PTSD, but also the man she knew as Lucas, the happy, funny guy she'd just been a bridesmaid for. The wonderfully warm human being whom she had come to like and love.

'Yes. And when our parents had their car accident and died, because Bill had been drinking heavily, Lucas turned to the only comfort he had left, because I'd not been there to help him. He took too much and overdosed and was rushed into A&E in Manchester. They found my details in his wallet and called me at London Saint.'

'That's why you disappeared so quickly.'

'Yes. I did look for you. I wanted to tell you, but you weren't in the department. You'd escorted a patient up to a ward and, though I wanted to wait and see you and explain, every second counted and I knew my brother needed me, so I just left. Without a word. Because he might have died and I wouldn't have been there.'

Maddy couldn't quite believe it. All this time she'd thought he'd left without a word because she wasn't important enough to him to have been considered. She'd been wrong the whole time!

'Lucas was barely alive when I got to Manchester and, once I was there, he was the only thing in my mind. Our parents were dead and I was grieving them and spending every minute by my brother's bedside, waiting for him to gain consciousness. And when he did, he was distraught and grieving, just like me. And more than anything he just wanted another hit to take the pain away. I watched him go through withdrawal and got him into rehab and I visited him every day, vowing never to let him down or leave his side ever again, in case he relapsed. I felt guilty that my leaving had contributed to his drug habit and I saw it as my job to get him off them.'

'It must have been terrifying for you.'

He nodded. 'It was. But slowly, week by week, Lucas started to get better. We went to counselling together to work our way through everything that had happened to us. We did a lot of work on ourselves and, by the time I felt strong enough to even think about what I had lost with you, so much time had passed I just felt it was probably better to just wipe the slate clean and leave you alone. I had no idea how much my going had affected you.'

'I was broken.'

'I know that now, but I didn't then. I thought staying away from you was for the best. That you'd find someone to settle down with, someone worthy. You'd always told me how you'd hoped to find someone special one day. Someone who would love you the way you'd never felt before. Someone who would choose you.'

She'd thought she had found that someone. She'd thought it was him. 'What happened with you and Lucas next?'

'I encouraged him to pursue his dreams. He'd always loved ice-skating and so I went with him to the rink so he could practise. I even paid for him to have a private coach and he finally started to have dreams and aspirations for his life. He applied for a job as an ice-dancer on a cruise ship and he got it, but he was terrified of doing it alone. I was only working as a locum in Manchester, so I offered to join the ship as medical crew to be with him.'

'That's amazing.'

'He made me make a promise, though.'

'Which was?'

'He wanted a fresh start. He wanted to be rid of his past and the only way he knew how to do that was to not tell a single soul about his addiction or past problems. He made me vow that I also would not tell a soul, ever.'

Now she began to understand. She'd told Nate about being attacked by a drug addict and he hadn't been able to tell her that his brother, the man for whom she was going to be a bridesmaid, was one. 'That's why you went to see him just now.'

'Yes. To ask for his permission to tell you. So I could explain to you why you never got all of me, why I held myself back. At first it was because I did not feel worthy of you. When you've spent your childhood being told you're worthless with nothing to offer, you start to believe it. And then I had the promise I'd made to my brother. I thought, if you knew, you'd be triggered by the revelation and refuse to be Lucas's bridesmaid, when I knew how much my brother liked you.'

She had tears in her eyes now. So much hidden pain, for both of them! 'You are worthy of love, Nate. You do have something to offer. I hope you know that.'

'Your love has made me see it and I hope that,

now I've been given permission to tell you everything, you will see that I stand here with my heart wide open to you and that I never meant to hurt you by holding back, but that I was afraid to give my all, in case it got rejected.'

'Oh, Nate!' She cradled his face with her hands and pressed her lips to his, hungry for his touch, hungry to be in his arms once again. She had felt bereft for so long!

'I thought *I* wasn't good enough,' she breathed, her forehead pressed to his. 'But it's always been you, Nathaniel. You've *always* had my heart. You're the only one who can hold it together and fix its broken pieces. If that's too heavy a burden, I'll understand, but know that I love you and want to be with you, and it doesn't matter about what Lucas used to be. He's not that now and I think it's time for *us* to find happiness.'

Nate nodded, smiling. 'I agree.'

'What do you say that we go back into that reception and show the happy couple how non-ice-dancers dance?'

Nate stroked her face. 'We will. But first… can you forgive me, for hurting you?'

She kissed him beneath the stars, in the middle of the ocean. 'Of course. Forgiven and forgotten.'

Maddy pressed her lips to his again, the man she loved in her arms at last. There were no secrets between them. All fears had been vanquished by the strength and the power of their love for one another.

EPILOGUE

NATE STOOD WITH his arm around Maddy on the harbour, watching as the large cruise ship *Amore* began its docking procedures. 'Excited?' he asked.

'To see Lucas and Carlos again? I can't wait!' She kissed his lips, gazing up at him.

He smiled. 'Me too. Think they suspect?'

'That we're going to get married whilst they're here? I hope not. I want it to be a surprise.'

'Well, Lucas can be quite wily, and he might wonder as to why I insisted that they both pack their dinner suits.'

She laughed. 'I'm ahead of you. I told them we were taking them to a theatre and then a very expensive and exclusive restaurant for a meal afterwards and they wouldn't be allowed in without black tie.'

'Clever! Are you nervous?' he asked, squeezing her to him, his hand at her waist, still unable to believe that this wonderful woman was going to be his wife in three short days.

'At getting married? Absolutely not. You?'

'Are you kidding me? I'd do it right now if we could.'

She chuckled and turned back to the ship, and waved at the sight of Lucas and Carlos waiting deckside for the gangways to be attached so they could disembark the ship onto Cyprus.

The island had become their home. After cruising around on *Serendipity* for their six-month contract, they had chosen the island as their favourite. Rich with myths and beautiful landscapes, green mountains and turquoise waters, the island was also filled with the sweetest, kindest people. They'd bought a stunning villa in Paphos in which to create their home together, whilst working in a clinic in the town. Here they planned to stay and raise their family, something he hoped they'd begin to work on after the wedding. He was ready and he knew that Maddy was too. It was all she dreamed of, a family of her own, and he'd promised to help her make one.

His idea was that Lucas could walk him up the aisle and Carlos could walk Maddy, as she had no family of her own to do so. It was going to be a small, intimate affair, just Lucas and

Carlos, and some of their other friends flying in tomorrow.

Everything was going perfectly. The best revenge to those who had once told him he was nothing was to live well, and he was exceeding that with Maddy by his side. Their relationship had gone from strength to strength.

'Hola!' Lucas ran towards them as he got closer and swung Maddy round in his arms as she squealed with happiness, letting go of her, only to hug his brother, clapping him on the back. 'Looking good, brother dear! Looking good!'

'You too. Hey, Carlos!' He gave his brother-in-law a hug. 'Welcome to Cyprus. How's things?'

'*Muy bien!* Good to see you. We have missed you! Madeline…' Carlos stood back to admire her in her beautiful white sundress. 'Stunning! You look amazing.'

Lucas nodded in agreement. 'Now, be honest, we're not just here for a little visit, are we?'

Nate tried to feign innocence. 'I don't know what you mean,' he said, smiling.

'You can't hide anything from me, brother dear! A little birdie tells me that plans are afoot…and it's not only the rock of Gibraltar that is huge, but also that diamond I see on Maddy's finger!' Lucas lifted Maddy's hand to admire the engagement ring Nate had slipped onto her hand months ago.

Nate laughed and shook his head. 'You don't miss a thing, do you?'

'So you are engaged?'

Nate looked at Maddy. 'Yes, we are.'

Lucas squealed with delight and pulled them both in for a hug. Carlos joined in too, determined not to be left out. 'When's the wedding?'

Nate looked at his watch and laughed. 'In three days. Fancy being a best man?'

Lucas let out another sound that possibly only could have been heard by bats and dogs at the upper end and then began flapping his hands in front of his face as he began to cry. 'I'm so happy for you guys! I hoped, of course, but didn't know for sure. You must be so happy!'

'We are,' Maddy said.

Nate turned to face Maddy and pulled her in for a kiss. 'I'm the happiest man alive.'

* * * * *

If you enjoyed this story, check out these other great reads from Lousia Heaton:

Nurse's Night Before Valentine's
New Year to Nine-Month Surprise
One Night to Twin Miracle
The Surgeon's Relationship Ruse

All available now!